D0855068

DEATH IN
VENICE, CALIFORNIA

DEATH IN VENICE, CALIFORNIA

Vinton Rafe McCabe

THE PERMANENT PRESS
Sag Harbor, NY 11963

Copyright © 2014 by Vinton Rafe McCabe

All rights reserved. No part of this publication, or parts thereof, may be reproduced in any form, except for the inclusion of brief quotes in a review, without the written permission of the publisher.

For information, address:
    The Permanent Press
    4170 Noyac Road
    Sag Harbor, NY 11963
    www.thepermanentpress.com

Library of Congress Cataloging-in-Publication Data

McCabe, Vinton—
    Death in Venice, California / Vinton Rafe McCabe.
       pages cm
    ISBN 978-1-57962-352-4
      1. Gay men—Fiction. I. Title.

PS3613.C328D43 2014
813'.6—dc23   2013040051

Printed in the United States of America

ACKNOWLEDGEMENTS

༄

I would like to express my appreciation to a lot of terrific people, all of whom made this book happen.

First, to NaNoWriMo, the National Novel Writing Month, whose challenge of completing a first draft in just one month was the genesis of this book. Undertaking that challenge taught me a new way of working: less second-guessing, more words on the page.

Second, to the Working Writers of Connecticut, and to the finest group of cohorts and critics I ever could have asked for. This novel had several midwives, Terri Garneau, Linda Strange, Wally Wood, Donna Renzulli, Don Blinebry, Kay Abella, Rick Newman, Kristen Bloom and Georgia Monaghan among them. Thank you all.

Third, to the folks at The Permanent Press, especially Marty and Judy Shepard. What a joy it is to find a publishing house that still believes in literature and still publishes it. Thanks to Lon Kirshner for the cover, and to Barbara Anderson, who makes the editorial process a pleasure.

And, fourth, to my friends, editors and publishers at The New York Journal of Books. To Rhonda and Ted Sturtz, who allow me to plunge headfirst into the world of books, authors and publishers on a regular basis and then express my opinion of it, and to Lisa Rojany Buccieri, who makes that opinion sound far cleverer, far wiser than it is.

I would also like to thank fellow writers Elizabeth Hilts and Stephanie Schorow for their sharp eyes and sharper minds. Your generous spirits contributed to this book more than you know.

And thanks to Benjamin Godfre, who is to Chase as Gielgud is to Hamlet.

And, finally, I want to acknowledge David Dumas for believing in this book when no one else (myself included) did. And for believing in me (and I in him) for these last thirty years. This book is for him.

—Vinton McCabe

ONE

∽

Jameson Frame had oatmeal for breakfast. With raisins and honey and a little cinnamon.

Jameson Frame ate slowly.

There was a time before his fortieth birthday, before he considered the power of words, of nouns, of proper names, syllable by syllable and letter by letter, when he was known simply as "James" and a time, years before that, when he had called himself "Jimmy."

At fifty, quite sure of the potency of vowels and consonants, harmoniously arranged, mellifluously spit out, he thought of himself always as "Jameson," even with raisins on his tongue.

He ate slowly, looking up and out at the horizon, at the point at which the sea met the sky. He had paid for the view, as he had the oatmeal, the coffee, and the fresh orange juice squeezed daily in the hotel kitchen, and he meant to enjoy it all with an equal and balanced fervor.

The balcony shifted suddenly from cool to hot as the California sun cleared the hotel wall, reflecting off the glass on the French door of his room to his left and making mirrors of many surfaces: sugar bowl, spoons, the fine silver line that circled the rim of cup and bowl and plate.

Frame moved his chin ever so slightly, lifting his eyes up and away from the glare. The sea, seemingly only inches away, became an undulating mirror of immense proportions as the day increased.

He closed his eyes against the light.

"I must buy myself sunglasses today. First thing today," thought Jameson Frame.

After his breakfast and his shower, he stood naked in the air-conditioned suite, in front of the full-length mirror in the passageway between his bedroom and bath. He appraised himself carefully, as if determining his value. Noted the slight underdevelopment of his chest and arms. Noticed the smoothness of his face and the soft curve of his abdomen. He was glad to conclude that both belied his age, carving off a few precious years. He looked to his skin that had been left uncovered and had just begun to blush from the California sun. He noticed each pockmark and blemish, each sag and tendril. Noticed what was graying and what was going missing. Noticed height and heft of his full form, which was tall, slim, if not particularly well toned. He measured the length of his legs and tested the texture of his elbows, where, when he pulled on the rough skin on the outside of the bend, arm extended out in front of him, the small flap now remained flaccid and no longer snapped back. He bent his elbow, arm up, slowly, watching the tightening of the skin.

Finally, he stepped to the mirror to look into his own eyes. They reflected his thoughts—his thoughts trapped in the amber of their pupils. They seemed to say, about his face, about his saggy, flat ass, about the changes in the patterns of hair growth all over his body, about his trip and this place, about where he had come from and where he wanted to be: *This is not what I meant at all. This is not it, at all.*

Suddenly cold in his immaculate room, he walked to the table beside the bed, reached down for his watch and fastened it onto his left wrist. It was a good watch, and costly, a treat he had once given himself, like this trip. A tip for the good service he had given to himself. It was the only jewelry he owned, his only bit of decoration. He put on fresh clothing: boxers, blue slacks, a fine leather belt, and a good Oxford shirt with the sleeves rolled only to just below the elbow. In a moment of inspiration, thinking: *When in Rome*, he slipped his bare feet into his soft shoes, leaving his socks, folded, where he had placed them earlier, before his shower, when laying out his clothes.

He walked to the window and threw open the curtains that he had closed when he had come in after breakfast, when he had determined that he had enough of the sun. Looking at the arc of the beach, now busy with people, dogs, skates, weights, kites, umbrellas, and surfboards, and looking out to the movement of the ocean beyond—vast water that suddenly seemed to be giving its permission so that the dry land might stay dry—he took an involuntary step backward. Transfixed by the sight, he backed to the corner of the bed and sat down, perched really, right on the edge, still looking out the glass, his heart seeming to beat with the pulse of the waves.

Jameson Frame was a collector. He bought and sold, as others do. But what he collected, what he bought with greed and sold with cunning, were words. He had had no small success as a writer, had won his prizes and taught enough classes to sell his own books and acquire the first editions of others. More than the books, though, more than the chafed leather covers, the brittle pages, the faded ink, he collected the words themselves. The meanings of them, yes, but also their rhythms, their colors, the taste of them as they rolled on his tongue. They resonated with him, echoed inside his heart.

Weeks before, while walking from his apartment on the Upper East Side on what had been yet another cold, gray morning in a long string of cold, gray mornings in New York, he had suddenly thought of some pointed words from Melville: *Whenever I find myself growing grim about the mouth; whenever it is a damp, drizzly November in my soul; whenever I find myself involuntarily pausing before coffin warehouses, and bringing up the rear of every funeral I meet . . .* It went on from there, playing out in his mind, unspooling verbatim from the text. But the ending, the ending of the thought was this: *I quietly take to the sea.*

Reaching the end of this memory play, his eyes cast up and left in recall, he realized that he had been somewhat somnambulant while considering Melville's advice on this greasy, cold, gray New York day that registered such a deep November in his soul. He found that he stood quite near the door of a coffee shop on a busy corner. The wind cut into his bones; the noise, his ears. He stood for a moment, his cold, red face close to the pink laminated menu that hung on the inside of the window, his breath fogging the glass. He scanned from Today's Special Tomato Soup to Chef's Salad to Baklava.

Entering, he swam through the warmth of the place, past the counter, past the glass case in which lemon pies with foot-high meringues endlessly spun, past the continual dull hum of conversation, to a small table from which a strip of wood-tinted plastic was peeling, away from the window. As he went, he unreeled the soft scarf from around his neck. He disengaged his hands from their gloves and unbuttoned his coat, all the while keeping his eyes fixed ahead on that small table. As he sat, a pink laminated menu appeared, along with a small glass of water with a few ice chips floating on the top. The glass was in fact, he noted, plastic.

Frame sat at the small table, facing front toward the counter, alert, as if taking notes.

To his left, two women sat away from the wall, toward the middle of the room. They talked of shopping, rustled their bags as they flipped through them, shifting tissue away from cheap cashmere from China. One slipped off her shoe under the table to rub at her heel while talking to her friend. He saw lipstick marks on her plastic glass. The other laughed and laughed and, because of her laughter, began to cough from some remnant of lingering flu.

Staring ahead, he saw a young man sitting at the counter, with legs dangling in a jingle-jangle manner, the right one in near constant motion. On the stool beside him was a backpack, whose strap he caressed with the tip of his fingers, again and again, making sure, always sure that it was there. On the floor below was a blue down-filled parka, left to fend for itself. The youth's hair was brown, in need of a cut. It had grown down to cover his collar. His shoulders were broad under a frayed wool sweater. He slumped forward as he circled his food, Today's Special Tomato Soup. Jameson ordered the same when asked. Ordered soup and a hot cup of coffee, as he kept watch on the young man, as he saw him crumple crackers into his bowl, as if the boy were sitting in his mother's kitchen. There was something touching, tender, in the simple action.

The fingers again grazed the backpack before the boy again lifted the spoon.

It is important to him, thought Jameson. *There is everything in there that matters to him.*

Who is he? Jameson wondered. A student? A fugitive? A traveler going to and fro upon the face of the earth?

He conjured Melville: *Almost all men in their degree, some time or other, cherish very nearly the same feelings towards the ocean with me.*

Was that it, then? Was this boy some fellow Ishmael in a gray November all his own?

He looked into the boy's face, through the mirror that hung in a sharp angle above the counter that would have showed a row of faces chewing in busier times, but now reflected only the slight movement of the boy's jaw, the vacant soft focus of his eyes as soup rose up and slid down, rose up and slid down with the occasional cud of a soggy fragment of cracker.

Frame could not quite bring himself to crumble the crackers into his own soup when it arrived in its heavy white bowl balanced on a plate, onto which had bled droplets of tomato. He studied his crackers, weighed them in his hand, then opened them, and bit off a corner of the hard, salty square before lowering it to the plate.

He considered the coffee, which he moved from the left of the soup to the right. Considered cream and sugar before leaving it black.

Things in place, he looked again into the mirror above the counter.

The boy ate, contented, his legs continuing their dance.

Looking down once more, Frame slowly wrapped his fingers around the base of the bowl. Felt the heat of it. Felt the heft of it as he lifted it from the plate. He slid it carefully across the side of the plate to scrape away any errant droplet of spilled soup. He brought his elbows out and then pressed them down onto the tabletop as he lifted the bowl up to his lips, as he looked into the steam, inhaled the scent of canned soup. As he took a small sip, he looked across the diameter of the bowl, again into the mirror above the counter.

His lips curled as he did this, perhaps from the heat of the soup.

In the mirror, he saw not the expected reflection of callow youth in repose, but, instead, the face, eyes, and jawline of the boy, all focused on him. Saw the taut neck, wary. Saw the eyes fixed, challenging, if not altogether angry, as if the boy had somehow realized himself the subject of surveillance.

Did the boy again finger the straps of the backpack?

The surface of the soup in his bowl shimmied as he set it down onto the plate and turned his sudden full attention to the wall to his right. To the Parthenon, to the Aegean, to the Isle of Crete, all of which were mashed together, without regard for specific geography or relative size, in blue on white, within the ever-present border of the Greek key, all on the plasticized wallpaper.

He lifted the coffee to his lips, and studied the Aegean, the Bosporus, the Dardanelles. He dreamed for a moment of the Colossus of Rhodes. The sea again, the sea.

TWO

ɷ

At that moment, Frame considered simple perpendicularity to be perhaps his chief accomplishment. He remained rigidly seated in the overheated restaurant.

In the front, the young man's legs jumbled. Trembled. Jumbled. He continued to glare at Frame in the mirror. Both faced front, the younger man looking backward.

Then, using his already moving legs as a means of propulsion, the boy leapt up, his hair flying out and around his face.

He allowed the weight of his body to carry him downward, nearly to the floor, so that he could, with one sweeping movement, gather his puffed coat and backpack close to him as he arose again. He looked a character in a farce standing there, his hair a vast cumulus, his eyes wide, his upper hand cupping the top zipper and the mesh of his backpack, his coat and pack's leather straps flopping outward.

He stood, glaring again. Some suddenness in his movement had dislodged his soup bowl, leaving blood on the counter. Frame saw the chunks of wet cracker. Felt a wave of nausea at the sight of it.

He raised his right hand to his throat, clutched the lump of his Adam's apple, as the boy suddenly made a movement toward him.

All the eyes in the place were on him, them, on the boy, who moved like a child on a lake who was just learning to skate, trembling toward him and at him, the tidy man, seated, who pressed what weight he had against the Aegean wall: pressing, pressing as if to disappear within the wet darkness of the sea.

The young man stopped five or six feet away from Frame's table. Stopped as if some force, some fear, had stopped him.

"No!" he said simply. Loudly. But his body trembled, his left hand extending in front of him, finger pointed like the barrel of a gun, thumb cocked to the side. With his other hand, he held his possessions as best he could, the slippery coat making its way to the floor.

By then his shirt had pulled up to his chest. Frame could see the line of soft down that led from his navel to his beltline and beyond. Could see the fine peppering of hair on the boy's thick chest, the rubbering of the angry muscles in his neck twisting as he stood snorting like a bull.

Having stood his ground and said what he had to say, the young man awkwardly began to back away. In a step or two, he turned his back on the older man.

Looking at him again in the mirror, Frame saw the boy shove his shirt down in his pants, saw him look again in the mirror and saw him again seeing Jameson watching him.

The boy's head slowly turned. He met Frame eye-to-eye, and looked at him, incredulous. There was almost a smile on his face as he stood by his stool, placed his goods on it and took his time, moving slowly, as if to say, "This is how I neaten up." He smoothed his shirt with flattened fingers, slowly putting on his puffed jacket; he carefully fitted his arms into the straps of the backpack and hefted it off the stool and onto his back.

Once more he looked Frame directly in the eye. Then he went quickly to the cashier stand, where the Greek woman who ran the place was only too glad to take his money. And off he went without a backward glance, the side of his puffed jacket smearing against the back of the door as it pushed him out.

Frame waved a hand in the air rather delicately and gave the waitress his uneaten bowl of soup. She accepted it without comment, and without comment brought him the lemon pie he ordered instead. She refilled his cup of coffee with an air of indifference, her expression a blank, as if wanting him to know that she refused to take sides.

His dessert at the ready with fresh fork and paper napkin, his coffee refilled, she retired to behind the counter.

He left the little coffee shop soon after, the tastes of sweet and bitter and acid on his tongue, mixed with the scent of lemon. He stood for a moment, making sure that he was quite alone, before turning again toward his own home, moving at his own pace, feeling the reassurance that again he remained not only perpendicular, but perfectly so, his body a straight, slim line as he moved, his reflection darting from pane to pane in the multiplicity of windows beside which he walked. Each new face, same smooth skin, same narrow blue eyes, reassured him, contributed to his wellbeing, as if each whispered the attribute it offered, as if the goods framed within were not for sale but for offer, freely, had he only the moment it would take to stop and pluck. Yet he moved on, feeling, deep within, some sense of failing, of frailty. Feeling once more the weight of it, the certainty of it: the *November in my soul*.

With the holidays coming, the days grew swiftly dark. None of the gloaming that midsummer gave to Central Park, times that were neither day nor quite yet night, but suspended, a time outside of time in which one could walk through a world tinged by the lightest blue; a time when there was time: time for another glass of wine, for lingering a bit more in conversation, hoping for one last good solid laugh. Time, it seemed, for another song, another embrace.

With the holidays coming, Jameson was faced with the certainty of his country home. A cabin really, to which he retreated with annual regularity in the days before Thanksgiving and stayed until well into the New Year. It was here, he said, that he went to escape the city. To unburden himself of the words he had gathered up throughout the length and breadth of the year. Words he would slowly commit to paper with the care of a calligrapher holding his finest brush, as he worked to open himself up onto the page.

His best work long past now, he knew his new work to be, more than anything else, his means to stage his annual escape, a way of confining the joys of the season to the Yule log on the television screen back in the den. Yet the house would be brimming with the warmth and light of the fireplace, with the bar well stocked, the kitchen as well, with Grace appearing each morning he was in residence to fix his breakfast, make a lunch for him that was left on the counter as she slipped out the back door, so as not to disturb his work. She would return again in the dusk with something hot—a casserole or mixed grill, which she set for him at the table in his dining room.

He would hear her in the kitchen as he ate. She kept the radio down low and moved gently among his things, setting and then clearing and cleaning and putting away, before she herself disappeared until the next day.

During those long nights in his cabin, Frame sometimes challenged himself, incited himself to put pen to paper or paper into the old Selectric on his desktop. He felt the thrum of it as he flipped the switch, running his fingers across the rubble of its case.

He seated himself behind the desk, his hands gripped to either side of the red typewriter. He urged himself, as he always did, to relax. Bade himself to breathe, only breathe, conjuring the words that had been said to him so often in his sickly youth. Believing that the words great and small that he had collected so assiduously lived within him, moved in and out with every breath, he felt at times like these, with something warm in his belly, a whisky in a cut-glass tumbler at his side, here, in his own house, at his own desk, in his own chair, that surely, surely the words would come. That he could wheeze them at last onto the paper, as his fingers flew and the typeset ball bounced in the machine.

But he sat, stroking the machine, his beloved pet, wondering about the time span that stretched out now until dawn.

Faced with the certainty of the red typewriter, Frame, standing on the street of the great gray city in the waning light of a day somewhere between All Saints and Advent, found himself quite suddenly caught up in the urge to write something down. He slapped the sides of his coat in search for a pen, a pencil, anything. He found a felt tip and a part of an old envelope. As he located his tools, his mouth was already at work, sorting out the sounds, marking meter, his tongue working as if to wet a mouth gone hard and dry. As soon as he found the envelope, he turned his shoulder to the world, and huddled himself in a doorway.

"I must escape," he wrote.

He looked at it, breathing hard. "Let it come," he whispered to himself. *Let it come. Let it come. Let it come. Let it come. Let it come. Let it come.*

His eyes flew upward, the glance of a hungry bird. He looked into the darkening sky, felt the need to hurry, hurry as night was coming fast.

He felt the movement of his heart, heard it. Heard the clicking of his own tongue as he tongued out sounds into words.

He added on, the ink shaping blue words: *I must escape by soaring.*

He was elated by the word: *soaring.* The idea of it. The rightness of that choice. The means of escape so pure, so right. Escape by lifting off and up, giving wing to his every idea of freedom.

Shaking, he kept writing, shaping blue words:

I must escape by soaring
Must not be held down
Oh, God, my mind's outpouring

Again, the breaking of the trance. Again the part of him that stood and looked over his own shoulder, eyes narrowed. *It's good.*

He wrote a last line before stopping. With bits of froth in the corners of his smiling mouth, he read it aloud in a whisper:

I must escape by soaring
Must not be held down
Oh, God, my mind's outpouring,
Just help me make the sounds

Well, that's not all of it, he thought to himself. But *'tis enough 'twill serve.* From here at least he would be working from a foundation. At least here was something to show for his day.

And it was *good,* if he could be the judge of these things on darkening city streets on cold afternoons.

It *was* good, wasn't it?

THREE

He brooded his way home. He felt the darkness almost a forewarning, as it gathered about him, swallowed the feet out from under him.

The sight of his townhouse soothed him after the onslaught of the city.

He'd come home empty handed. He had had awful pie instead of finding the book he'd gone out to buy.

Frame took off his coat, slid the scarf from his neck and pushed it into the left sleeve and hung it away in the hall closet. He opened the pocket doors and walked into his front room. He stood behind his father's old wingback chair for a moment, his right hand on the highest point of the chair's back, as if the old man were in it still. As if he and the others of the lineage still sat, awaiting the photographer's flashbulb before they could move once more.

And so, for the moment, he felt himself lost in time, as if the subject of one of the portraits in the hall.

He sat in the great wingback chair then, reclaiming it as his own.

Jameson Frame was, to the eyes of the world, a successful man. His was a success that mixed, however mildly, with celebrity.

The notoriety that he had—the sort that, from time to time, earned him an invitation to come and be a part of a round-table discussion on a public television show, or demands for his attendance at certain charity events or occasional dinner parties or speakers' nights at Upper West Side Ys or readings at some of the larger libraries—was satisfactory to him. He had, in younger years, when his fame was fresher, reveled in it. (Had he, at that time, had Google to play with, he would have most certainly known the number of hits his name could attract on the average day.)

Surprisingly, Frame's reputation as a man of letters was based on only three volumes published, two of which had happened early on. His first, *Pennyweight*, had been largely allegorical and altogether humorless. In it, he made use of the concept of the value of things to open the minds and hearts of his readers to any of several liberal social and political causes through a hard turnip of a novel that likely would have disappeared had anyone else written it.

But, being who he was, the teller of family tales, the wanton scion, the sole discordant note played loudly against the smooth sound of banking that had, until then, been the music of the household, the book became something of a smash.

And so the boy rebel, just fresh from college in New Haven, Connecticut, found himself to be considered a rather tasty morsel, if only briefly.

Jameson, then Jimmy, had only written the book as a means of waving his literary arms and attracting his father's attention.

Given that as a boy he had come home on time as always from second grade only to find his father walking briskly, with suitcase in hand, down the cascading staircase toward the front door and, given that when he asked the father, "Where are you going?" he was told, "I am going out and never coming back!" it seemed a reasonable enough thing to seek.

Indeed, his father never had come back. He never walked into that house again. He had, instead, abandoned the boy to his mother, Penelope, whose intimates sighed her name softly to her when near and called her "Penny" behind her back.

No matter the many times that Penelope proved that she was the reason that his father had been driven from the house—no matter how many "uncles" appeared at the door after dinnertime, with liquor on their breath, no matter how many other "fathers" she would supply him with (five, all told, one a General)—Frame believed that, had he not come through the door just when he did, his father would have stayed at home.

The boy with no father—or with too many, depending upon the point of view—would not see his own again for many years. He would have to content himself with picture postcards and occasional birthday wishes. On his fifteenth birthday, he shook hands with his father and began what would become a ceremony of unremitting guilt which would garner for him not only the cost of the world's best education, but also a reasonable enough income (for one who had suffered through life with various other "fathers" and "siblings," some of whom were vaguely related by blood or marriage, others not at all, but all of whom smelled rather oddly and behaved outrageously) and, ultimately, the outright ownership of the New York townhouse.

Penelope, who had been given the right to live in it for life, had, some years before, slipped drunkenly into the swimming pool at her house in the Hamptons and out of this life. Her husband at the time, some sort of a dowager prince, had been questioned and released. The house, a summer rental, was of no importance, although Jameson had rather kindly stood his semi-siblings the cost of the rest of the lease before letting them know, via his very good attorney, that they would no longer be welcome in the townhouse.

Indeed, that townhouse figured rather centrally to the tale told in his second book, *The Antecedents*, his rather exhaustive and thoroughly sordid retelling of his family history. Not content to simply repeat the means by which "Lobster Frame" had been given its name in one of the better restaurants of the *belle epoque*, Jameson dug deep into the family vaults to uncover Freemasons, suffragettes, and followers of Guy Fawkes.

This new volume, profusely illustrated with the very portraits that still formed the timeline that was the front hallway, was published just as his father was slipping from coherence in an excellent hospital that still today bears his name for its neurological wing. Those attending the father often remarked as to how very kind the young Mr. Frame was to come and visit his father so frequently and to read to him from the pages of the book of their joint family history. And, they remarked, his smiling, almost glowing face, as he read aloud from the massive manuscript nearly filled the room with light.

It is said that just as Jimmy Frame was reading how his great-great-great-grandfather gave the Skull and Bones its very first skull, his father, who had been slapping the air only moments before, seemingly defending himself from invisible flies, slipped away, allowing his hand to slide to the floor as he did so.

It was some years before Frame wrote again.

He took over the running of the townhouse and oversaw the redecoration of the place—the restoration, as he called it, because all traces of his mother, all the flounces, peony prints and shags, were wrested from the place, and replaced with hard lines and hard woods.

He took a job at a small but good enough college that, admittedly, did not involve a great deal of work.

He wore bow ties during an era of open collars and chest hair, gold chains and turtlenecks.

And he grew accustomed enough to the roundtable discussions on public television shows, so much so that no less than Gore Vidal, perhaps irate over the fact that Jimmy Frame knew to smile his little cat smile when issuing *bon mots*, warned him in a hiss to "settle his fat ass down."

He attained some things and acquired others. Avoided marriage and other entanglements, partially by rushing away to his cabin when required. He developed an air of quiet sophistication and the delicate paunch of the puritan born.

He began writing poetry. Verse, really, as the things he wrote tended to rhyme.

With the years passing and no more fathers to punish—the blood one was dead, the faux ones broke—on the eve of his fortieth birthday he gathered together a slim volume of poetry and, with the assistance of the university press of the extraordinary school that he had once attended and to which he had been so loyal and generous over the years, saw it published on very nice paper, with a silk ribbon sewn in as a bookmark.

To his great surprise, the little volume, *On Scrimshaw and Others*, was nominated for several awards, one or two of which were sufficiently well known that Grace, who was at the time a new employee, congratulated him and seemed duly impressed.

On Scrimshaw and Others went on to win a few of the smaller awards for which it had been nominated. (The sort that had only the states' names in them.)

For states west of the Mississippi, he sent only a letter of thanks and did not attend the award banquet. These were not enough to secure him a position at a top-flight university, but enough to again secure him the second or third chair at public television roundtable events.

It was on one of those shows that Jameson once quipped that he was seriously considering revising the text of *On Scrimshaw and Others* and rereleasing it under the new title, *Snubbed,* to the general amusement of the table.

Sitting in his great chair in the front room of his townhouse, his feet resting, crossed at the ankles, on a very fine tufted pouf in front of him, Frame took from his pocket the poem he had begun.

Doggerel, he thought as he read through it again, what with *soaring* and such. And he wadded the envelope up in the ball of his hand.

He leaned back once more into the soft down of the chair. He stared at the dark crimson of the walls, the enclosing walls.

Slowly, slowly, he smoothed out the paper once more, looking at the blurred blue writing, making sure that it was still legible. Were it not, he would need to copy it quite quickly, as it was slipping from his mind.

With the sensation that perhaps, just perhaps, all that was best and finest and funniest and saddest and most hopeful was not all in the past, Frame, not unlike that mad-eyed boy in the coffee shop, bolted from his chair. The little envelope upon which his wishful poem was written fluttered to the floor.

"No!" he said.

His arm was out, stretched out in front of him, his finger and thumb like the shape of a gun. *No!* he thought again, as he hurried from the room, up the stairs and sought out his best suitcase and the clothes he would need for warm-weather travel.

FOUR

∽

Jameson Frame was flummoxed, both by the airport and the crowd, and as well by the lights, and the smells, and the noise that echoed and rolled like the roar of an ocean. And so he tightened the thin curve of his lip ever so slightly into something resembling a vaguely amused moue and squinted into the distance.

He had waited on line in the first-class lane, looking, to his mind, perfectly at ease within the rather repellant hodge-podge of humanity. He navigated as best he could the maze of straps and poles that were meant, apparently, to allow him to gather himself to the counter at the zigzagged front of the line. There, he stood, quietly atwitter, on the painted thick red line, waiting to be summoned ahead by the clerk.

After two rather embarrassing non-starts, when Frame had become thoroughly convinced that the clerk was beckoning him onward with an errant twitch of an eyebrow, he was finally instructed verbally to "Get moving" after several similar twitches and a wave of the hand failed to cause him to sally forth a third time.

Once at the counter and in the hands of the Jim-Bob behind it, cards and slips of paper were exchanged, Frame's superb calfskin suitcase was surrendered and checked and, with the clerk sticking the thumb of his back-stretched arm by way of the requested direction, Frame set out to find his jet.

He shuddered his way through security and tried to count, with his eyes, the number of coins that he had removed from his pockets to make sure that the same were returned. Gathering his change, his exquisite watch and his dignity, he stepped away from the security area and, spotting a national chain ahead, treated himself then to what he hoped would be a fine and cheering cup of *café con leche*.

The coffee unfortunately was bitter.

After a sip or two, Frame left the emporium and, instead, bought himself some chewing gum to help keep his ears from compressing inward during the flight, as well as the morning's newspaper. And made his way down to the "concourse."

He twisted the word around on his tongue and in his mind. "Concourse." The very thought of it, the trampling of its intended meaning. The *concours* of the learned where men, draped in the perfect robes that gave soft witness to their status, gathered in public to discuss art and literature and the news of the day. That *concours* to this *concourse*, this bus station with pretentions, smelling of fried foods and damp air-conditioned chill, even in the onset of winter.

The concourse was, in this airport, a cul de sac of sorts, a place from which three planes would embark, one of them Frame's. While blessedly early enough before the holiday season, sparing Frame the jostling that is inevitable when happy travelers bear gift packages like shields and spears, the concourse was still filled with the piped cheery sounds that serve a preamble to the season. Not quite carols as yet, but the collateral sounds of the seasonal muzak.

Frame found his gate. He located his ticket and made sure that the information presented by the one matched the other. He then sought a seat in the overcrowded forum. Attempting to avoid those who stroked, stared at, listened to or otherwise enjoyed free interplay with devices of any sort, whether tethered to their body with various cords or not, Frame soon found himself winding his way to the very edge of the crowd and to the seats that were wedged right under the far wall, away from the over-large window and away from the gate itself.

While the distance caused him no small amount of worry, he decided that this was indeed the better place to sit, as it allowed him the ability to look out over the crowd without becoming an actual part of it.

And so he sat, casually yet with his head held high, as if expecting a butler any moment who, with a perfectly clean white linen towel draped over his arm, would announce tea.

Across from him sat two young men. They wore the same casual attire of many in this day, clothing that could have suited a twelve-year-old nicely. Frame looked at them with their matching baseball caps, their sneakers and cotton twill pants. He felt a momentary rush of content-ment, seeing them, two young men, so very taken with each other's com-pany. Their body language betrayed a casual intimacy, of the sort that youth all too often takes for granted.

The two laughed loudly, talked fast. They fought over every posses-sion, from their game box to their tiny music player. As one fastened the tiny plugs within his ears, the other tugged and tugged on the cord, shrieking, "Give me, give it to me," until, laughing, the unit was surren-dered and the battle rejoined over the next trinket.

They seemed like puppies, careless, playing at biting.

Amused, Frame slowly leaned back into his chair, until his shoulder blades met the seat back. He raised his recently acquired newspaper, to be able to survey the scene more comfortably without being noticed.

He thrilled himself by plucking from midair the words from 2 Samuel: *very pleasant hast thou been unto me: thy love to me was wonderful, passing the love of women*. David mourning the loss of his great love, Jonathan.

How like these two, thought Frame. Watching the two intertwined completely, enthralled with each other, calling to each other in great whoops of joy. Watching the eyes of the one burn with lust for the other.

And yet, something jarred him. Something untoward in the skin.

Frame saw how the skin of one accordioned against the smooth, taut flesh of the other. How, when the one leaned his arm up against his friend's ribs when they jostled playfully, he experienced what could only be thoughtfully considered a sort of "slippage" of the dermis.

When he pressed his arm playfully against the other's chest, his arm quivered and the skin seemed to slip for a moment away from the bone. And when he was jostled back, there seemed a great waddle formed from the flesh of his arm that, for many a moment, swung loose before remem-bering its rightful attachment.

Frame dropped his newspaper in a moment of confusion. He retrieved it very slowly, with his head down but his eyes looking upward, from which vantage point he could see quite clearly now that what had appeared to be two young men was in fact two men of different genera-tions and that the one whose eyes burned when they looked at the other was indeed far older.

How inappropriate then was his hat?

His tee shirt—stretched tight though it was against a hardened chest—was ridiculous, as were his sockless tennis shoes. More ridiculous still was his behavior, his noisy, intrusive ways, which seemed to call out: *Look at me, please look at what I have!*

How strange that he was the only one who noticed. Or had all these others, noticing sooner the vulgar display, simply turned away, already and sooner?

Was Jameson Frame the last to know?

Still very slowly in the somewhat theatrical action of gathering together the disparate parts of his newspaper, he attracted the attention of the older of the men, who, by way of greeting Frame, took off his cap and nodded his head forward. And Frame was sure that he saw the too-thick, too-glorious results of dye and hair restorative surgery. It appeared to him that the man wore a second hat underneath the cap—this one carefully constructed of grafted and ever-so-carefully tinted hair. His coif was cut boyishly, and tippled into his eyes as he bowed his head. The tips of it were strangely blonded, as if dappled by a most cooperative sun.

Beneath the bangs, Jameson saw the man's face very clearly, as he had come, in his courtly bow, irritatingly close to Frame's own face.

The man's eyes were an uncanny, unnatural blue and the area around them very smooth, as if the man had never ever creased his eyes with a smile, or worried his forehead with a frown.

Indeed, his entire face had a feline cast and the skin seemed very tight and, at the same time, very very tan.

At his throat he wore a golden chain, at the end of which was a single golden letter, the letter "T."

At this point, Frame willed himself to look away, using the downward motion of his eyes to guide him to, at last, notice and gather up the last bits of the newspaper and pull them into his lap.

"L.A?" the ghoulish man asked.

"L.A?" Jameson echoed, uncomprehending. Then, after a pause, "L.A. Why, yes, L.A."

"That's where we're going, too," said the tinted corpse. His companion, whose chest was as rounded and ripe with youth as his elder's was a blow against nature, bobbled his head eagerly, his own golden, soft natural locks falling into his own naturally blue blue eyes.

Jameson willed himself to ask: *Is this your son?*

But did not, could not. And so he put his attention quite solidly back on his newspaper, lifting it again, this time covering quite completely the whole of his face.

He inhaled the clean scent of the newsprint and closed his eyes against the memory of the Ghoul. From somewhere inside of him came a deep shudder, as again, against the screen of his inner eyelids, played the image of the man's cartoon blue eyes, his flawless tight skin, pulled too tight against his cheeks, his teeth alarmingly, supernaturally white against the tan. His teeth the rictus gateway to his miasmic breath and his ancient, turgid stomach.

The whole of the Ghoul seemed unnatural, as if the illusion that was his youth and vigor had resulted from bathing in the blood of infants, leaving Frame to wonder if the hills of Southern California were somehow the home of vampires who basked in the sun.

FIVE

∞

Resplendent in his first-class seat, Jameson Frame still pondered sunshine, the specific and wondrous sunshine of California beaches. Having no interest in West Coast celebrities, he had, when making his plans, chosen to steer clear of Malibu, and of any of the beachside communities in which one might see the latest action hero running along the beach. He seriously considered, for a brief moment, the idea of instead going to Carmel-by-the-Sea where, he had been told, there were some quite good art galleries to be visited and some excellent cuisine to be had, to say nothing of the stilt houses that were constructed precariously over the sea, and, of course, Pebble Beach. But because of its location halfway up the California coast, and because of the warning given him by his travel agent of morning fogs and cold nights and, in the end, because he did not intend to run from cold to cold and damp, he drifted away from the notion. It had sounded good. And then, when he looked at the map of Southern California with his spontaneous hope of finding someplace in the sun in which he could hide away fading, his eye was caught by a single word. *Venice.*

Not the Venice of his youth, to be sure, of his graduation trip to Europe in which he and a few choice friends Eurailpassed from town to town, arriving at last at that place both sacred and profane, Venice. Calling forth the memory of it now brought to mind Waugh and *Brideshead* and a single pristine thought: *I was drowning in honey, stingless.*

Charles Ryder certainly had said this.

Why do the drab get all the good lines?

Sebastian would not have noticed, only enjoyed and imbibed. And drowned all the faster and more willingly because of it.

The fuller quote now issued from somewhere in the back of his mind: *The fortnight at Venice passed quickly and sweetly—perhaps too sweetly; I was drowning in honey, stingless. On some days life kept pace with the gondola, as we nosed through the sidecanals and the boatman uttered his plaintive musical bird-cry of warning . . .*

How perfect, thought Frame, *to be keeping pace with the gondola . . .*

He closed his eyes against anything that might rob him of this, his own sweet, vague memory of that peculiar time and place, as overlaid against Catholicized fiction.

Venice. The murk, the old, khaki waters slopping slowly up against the smooth marble, *The Stones of Venice*.

"Ahhhhhhh . . ." breathed Frame. *Ruskin, too.*

Waugh and Ruskin and Frame. And Venice.

In the travel agency, he'd pointed at the map, at that word, at *Venice*. "Here," he said, "I will go here, to this place." And he booked his flight and he booked his room in the best hotel in the suite with the best view of the ocean and he began immediately to dream of the Palazzo Ducale, that which Ruskin called, "The central building of the world."

The embodiment of the city.

Of *Venice*.

He felt sleepy with the efforts of memory, youth overlapping age, overlapped by the age of the city itself, old when Ruskin visited, older now, sinking, smelling, rapt and divine.

He felt again the cradle of the soft chair within the coffin of the gondola, and heard again the gondolier, not singing, but wheezing with effort, and muttering to himself as he worked to move the craft forward in the dark, thick muck.

And yet, his own arms safely tucked in, across his narrow chest, his body, for the most part, dry, except for the occasional baptism that is unavoidable when one is rocked by the simple motion, by the slow propellant of long-muscled human arms moving a long wooden paddle against the listless canal water, the slow flow of it given just a bit of torque by bits of the tide, from where the canal met the sea. He drifted then and drifted now, remembering it.

"Oh, hi!" said a voice. Something tenor and silly, with a nasal tone that pushed too hard. "Hello! Oh, look who's here."

Frame opened his eyes, his left palm arising to shade his face from the harsh overhead light and saw the two men from the concourse.

They walked down the aisle and then took two seats in the row oppo-site. The old one looked over at Frame in feline delight. "We always wait until everyone else is on board. I cannot bear to stand in line. I like to feel free to get up and move around."

"Ah," said Frame, who had himself rushed to the line as soon as the plane was called as a means of separation from these two.

The Ghoul, Frame noticed, had a voice that burbled out of his ridicu-lously pink lips with a tinge of an accent. One that reminded him of Lau-rence Olivier in his latter years, when his performances tended toward grandiose, sawing the air and issuing accents just like this, that Middle European sound so vague as to be Vienna by way of Panama. A sound one could hear and hear and never decide: *Is this man a foreigner trying still to be perfectly understood, despite the handicap of foreign birth, or is this a man from Ohio who seeks to set himself apart by virtue of an alien nasality of his own design?*

Frame decided upon Ohio and snorted at the thought.

He realized a moment too late that he had, in weighing these options, failed to close his eyes as he most surely should have, but, instead, had been staring straight ahead into the bulging eyes of the Ghoul, who seem-ingly had mistaken his brief trance for interest.

"My name is Tobin," he said with a bit of a giggle. "But feel free to call me Toby. Just Toby. So American it sounds. But what is one to do?" He shrugged his shoulders and tipped his head toward the seat next to him. His jaw nudged forward. His eyes enlarged, bulged a bit. Jameson, looking directly at them for the first time, found them lifeless, the eyes of an animated corpse.

The Ghoul nudged his younger companion, who, heretofore, had been looking out the window, seemingly fascinated by the tarmac. "This is my good friend Kyle."

Kyle turned by way of brief greeting. He turned his face fully toward Jameson, not nodding, not speaking, as if the sight of him should suffice.

The perfection of the man, as now Frame had been issued a formal invitation to look upon him, to take his time—the golden nature of him, with the glow of his wheaten hair moving forward and down, into his eyes, his perfect teeth, his stubbled cleft jaw, his wonderful, solid neck that disappeared into his collar—all seemed supremely and utterly alive, even in repose. As if perhaps the vampire Ghoul employed the youth to allow him, from time to time, to sap him a bit of his life's blood. Not enough to leave a mark, to make a circle under the eyes or cause a wrinkle to form on the brow or the hair to thin by even a single follicle, but still enough, just enough to sustain the Ghoul as the darkened mirror image of this resplendent youth that he was.

There was a power in the young ones, thought Frame, *a power that, indeed, only the youthful possess. So that if he would say, "Stay," one would most assuredly stay. And if he said "Go" one would leave soon after.*

Frame waited for a breath or two. For the youth to issue orders. But the boy only looked at him through the warm waters of his eyes.

And Frame, in that moment, said the thing that came into his mind. The quote, one of his own, framed the image that filled his own lonely eyes:

Ah, but,
Youth has only youth to offer.

He was incredulous at first that he had said the thing aloud.

The young man, hearing it, looked back to the tarmac, as if he had taken umbrage.

The Ghoul gave a gasp.

The Ghoul pursed his lips, perhaps in indignation, but then attempted to spread them into something of a grin.

"I've read that poem a thousand times!" he said, excited.

"Ah," said Jameson Frame, caught by the words issued from his own mouth. The line, one of his favorite lines from what had, otherwise, been one of his lesser works, one of the "Others" from *On Scrimshaw and Others*:

Youth has only youth to offer.

A melancholy thing, that. But borne out a million million times when Frame had had to face the new semester's class, all dithering about one thing or another, or when watching young people at society weddings, where the young men inevitably take off their tuxedo jackets and roll up their sleeves while dancing and sweating into their starched collars.

It seemed so obvious when he had written it down, only a jot, only a notation, nothing profound.

And yet the wounds, the bleeding it had caused. The young so sensitive about the fact that, aside from tight skin, ample hair and roving eyes, as well as the syrup that seems to naturally fill them from head to toe, that they have really nothing very interesting to say when you come face to face with them, in classrooms, in restaurants, even in bed.

The Ghoul was making spidery fingers at him, as if trying to conjure. With a sudden, bright light of recognition illuminating his eyes, he said, "Why you're Jameson Frame, aren't you? You wrote that. I saw you on Charlie Rose, I remember."

Damn you and damn PBS, thought Jameson Frame.

At this moment, the stewardess interrupted to call all passengers' attentions to the card in the pocket in front of them. Frame studied the card with an intensity of someone holding a potentially winning lottery ticket. He stared only at the card.

For a moment, his eyes flicked up and to the left to see that the Ghoul was still very much focused on him. With his gnarled hand (upon which rested a very fine golden crested ring), he gestured and his head nodded. As if to say, "I haven't forgotten. We'll continue this later." He batted his plucked, dyed eyebrows at Jameson Frame like a Southern belle with an empty dance card.

Frame felt exhausted suddenly and quite trapped, as the doors of the jet slammed shut and the plane began slowly to propel itself down the runway, building momentum as it went.

SIX

∞

It occurred to Jameson Frame that if he simply moved inward one seat, he might flee the Ghoul by staring out the window with a mien of intense interest, in a manner similar to Kyle's. And yet, when he somewhat ceremoniously slid to his right, it seemingly indicated to the gleeful Ghoul that Frame was, in moving to the window, meaningfully clearing the aisle seat, making space, and issuing something of an invitation.

And the older man, all in a moment, seemed to vaporize from his own seat and appear next to Frame, putting his face as far into his personal space as the armrest would allow.

The Ghoul squeezed Frame's left arm with his spidery, veined hand and issued something of a giggle mixed with a sigh as he again turned his attention to the front just in time to see the stewardess competently close the loop of a shortened seatbelt in front of her chest before she returned to the front galley.

The Ghoul, after generally twittering for a moment, turned to Frame and issued a vast and raucous torrent of praises—literary, political, intellectual, and personal. These were followed by a volley of questions that seemed primed to rip from Frame not only the last shred of his personal privacy, but his dignity as well.

In the meanwhile, Kyle, first sensing and later fully determining the Ghoul's absence by finally turning his head ever so slightly away from the window, responded by turning around, lifting the armrest gently upward and then sliding his muscular form so that his head rested against the far point of the headrest by the window, with the rest of him unfurling into the vacated seat.

How wonderful he looked, even when turned away, even when supine. Frame attempted to see the rise and fall of his chest, but could not. He could only see a bit of sunlight on his yellow hair.

Trapped, Frame attempted to charm the cagey old Ghoul by using with him the same manners and anecdotes that he usually reserved for the person on his right at charity dinners. He told the old man the tale of the time that he, Jameson Frame, had managed to visit the Bush ranch in Texas for barbeque, thanks to a connection from New Haven and an ill-formed belief on the part of the Bush election committee that he would be good for a sizeable check. The brisket, it turned out, was mediocre, as was the amount written on the check.

The Ghoul's eyes grew wide at the tale. He oooooohhhed a minty vowel and asked what Laura had worn.

Frame told him this and much, much more. The tale of John Kennedy Jr. who had once attended a party at Frame's brownstone. The tale of that actress—whose name Frame could never remember, which inevitably led to a guessing game in which those to whom the tale was told would finally guess her name, joyfully—who walked over to Frame's table at a very well known, very celebrated restaurant (whose name was the same as a man's first name, the name of the owner's son, as was well known to people who know these things) and, by way of rather effusively greeting him, called him "Mr. Capote." And, of course, from the tales of the many roundtable television discussions, the story of the rudeness on the part of Gore Vidal.

The Ghoul, who had been clutching various parts of Jameson Frame's body throughout his presentation of anecdotes, issuing from time to time a squeak sounding something like, "Oh, my!" or "You don't say!" now almost exhaustedly clutched Frame's forearm once more.

"You mean he actually told you to settle your fat ass down?"

"Quite. Or he would 'settle it for me.'"

"An awful man."

"Dreadful."

"But talented," said the Ghoul after a beat.

"Yes, talented."

"Undeniably talented."

"True. So true."

Appearing quite dazzled, the Ghoul looked back a bit longingly to his old seat.

"I suppose I should slip back . . ." he said.

"Oh, yes, surely."

"Just to check on Kyle."

"Mustn't let him wake alone."

"No."

"No."

"It's been amazing talking with you."

"Very nice. Very enjoyable all around."

The Ghoul appeared to be gathering his skin around him to make his departure. He turned suddenly, thrust his hand into his pocket, and said, "Here's my card. You must let me be of any help to you that I can while you are in Los Angeles. Dinner, company, companionship. Let me know if I can be of help to you in any way."

"Ah, how very kind."

And Frame made a show of placing the card given him into the top pocket of his sports jacket.

"Well, I hope we have the chance to speak again," said the Ghoul, rising at last.

"I am most certain that we will," said Frame, rising just slightly before returning his head and neck to the curve of the seat.

He closed his eyes for a moment to feign fatigue and opened them slightly a moment later to watch the Ghoul, back at his seat, slither in beside the tranquil Kyle.

Frame stretched his arms as best he could out in front of him, issuing a sigh of his own with the effort. He twisted his chin onto the palm of his right hand, his head into the soft headrest and soon enough joined Kyle in a state of tranquil slumber.

The Ghoul, for his part, feeling the calming warmth of Kyle's body touching him here and there, assumed the posture of a chipmunk dining on a seed, as he recalled the anecdotal feast he had just attended.

Frame awoke to the cradling motions of the plane. He sat up, quite upright, to see what was happening. He looked first out the window to see that they were already flying over a vast landscape of buildings with the ocean, the endless ocean, churning in the distance.

A sense of giddiness came over the passengers as various gongs and lights alerted them to return to their seats, fasten their seatbelts and prepare for arrival.

While moving his head quickly enough to avoid eye contact, Frame scanned the seats across and one row up from him, saw Kyle standing and taking a carry-on bag down off the rack above. Saw the Ghoul gesticulating, guiding him, and, at the same time, using one arm to protect himself from the possibility that that baggage might come crashing down on top of him.

Neither seemed particularly interested in Frame, who, for his part, slipped his sports coat on and sat, his personal belonging in hand, ready to disembark at the first possible opportunity. Involuntarily, his right hand flew up to the pocket over his heart and felt that the card that the Ghoul had given him was still inside.

Seeing this, the Ghoul smiled, and, with his hands, pantomimed the act of dialing a telephone, while, with his mouth, sounded out an overly dramatic "Call me!"

He winked then at Frame as he and Kyle pushed past, attempting to be the first off the plane. Frame, for his part, gave them and all others a wide berth, allowing all to hurry past, while he calmly waited for the explosion of disembarkation to complete itself.

He made his way quite slowly down to the baggage area, expecting that there would, right there waiting for him, be a man with a sign. And upon that sign would be his name, Jameson Frame.

There always was, at all times, on all such trips, always one of these men in every airport to which Frame traveled. And this man, who always wore a black jacket and cap, no matter his age or build, would always say to him, "Good day, Mr. Frame. Did you have a good flight?" He would always then ask for the baggage receipts and would always, after lifting up that wonderful calfskin bag, say, "This way, Mr. Frame," and take the bag and Frame to the long black car (always a long black car) that waited for them. Then he would open the car door, bidding Frame enter and closing it silently as the passenger perused the backseat bar.

At LAX, Frame stood, his baggage claim at the ready in his right hand, and scanned the crowd of men in black hats who awaited their fares. He looked from man to man, less taking in their faces than the names that they had printed on the cards upheld in front of them.

Seeing no placard with his name on it, puzzled, he approached the sole black hat who held no card. And he whispered to the man, expectantly, "Jameson Frame."

The stocky, muscular man with a darkly whiskered skin, said nothing. He took the baggage claims without comment and neither indicated that Frame should follow nor that he should stay where he was. And so Frame waited, very quietly, very appropriately, right where the two had met.

After waiting very patiently for some minutes, Frame happened to notice his wonderful calfskin bag was over by the front door, in the left hand of the man who had taken his baggage claims. The man was looking directly at Frame with a somewhat irritated look on his face. As soon as Frame turned and began to walk toward the door, the man walked through it and out to the parking lot.

Without a gesture, without a word, he walked rapidly to the car, forcing Frame to briefly run after him to catch up.

The man put the suitcase in the trunk and opened Frame's door for him before walking around and getting into the driver's seat.

Frame got in, settled himself and closed his own door after himself. He looked up and saw the man's dark, angry eyes looking directly at him.

"Well?"

Frame looked puzzled. "Pardon?" he at last managed.

"Where to?" said the man, pronouncing each word quite separately.

Frame gave the man the name of his hotel in Venice. The moment the words came out of his mouth, the car roared to life and sped out of the lot.

The man drove briskly. He made no conversation of the sort that Frame was accustomed to by drivers who always wished to know the nature of his visit, the quality of his flight.

Instead, this man spoke to himself, in a low but violent manner. Frame could not be sure but suspected that the man was speaking a foreign tongue, one that seemed quite like gibberish to him.

Alarmed at the possibilities this presented, Frame attempted to make conversation with the man, having once read a book that instructed those who were about to be abducted to try, in every means possible, to get the abductor to see his target not as simply a target, but as a living, breathing human being.

"So lovely here . . ." Frame said vaguely as they hurdled along. *Was that a palm tree in the distance?*

The man made no answer, but snarled a little snarl and set his jaw as the car sped up.

The motion of the car tipped Frame to and fro. And with every jerking, lurching motion of this vehicle, with every screech of its brakes as the madman at the wheel drove up to the tailpipe of the car in front of him and then braked in the moment before impact, Frame became more vividly, more terrifyingly filled with a sense of peril.

Somewhere in the bowels of Los Angeles, Frame noticed the man making a sudden turn. Not onto the next highway, as expected, but onto a long, flat roadway called "Palms Boulevard."

"Now, surely," said Frame, letting his irate nature step in front of his natural fear, "surely we should have gotten on the 405!"

He got no answer from the front of the car.

"I said where is the 405!" Frame declared, gesticulating wildly.

"Sit back and let me drive!" the driver demanded, and the car flew faster down the road.

The man wove through traffic, muttered, raged, spat, and, at last, pulled up with an astonishing screech of his tired brakes, in front of the Hotel des Bains in Venice.

"Get out." The man said to Jameson Frame.

And Frame got out of the rear right seat as the man exited through the front left. The driver looked around, alert, is if searching for something nearby. He hurried to the trunk and took out Frame's calfskin suitcase, tossing it roughly onto the curb.

Seeing this, the doorman of the Hotel des Bains approached the bag and touched it gently, as if searching for bruises. Lifting the whistle he wore hanging from a tasseled cord around his neck, he turned his face as if to remonstrate the driver.

Suddenly, as if startled by something, the driver ran to the car door that he had left open, jumped into the car, slammed the door hard behind him and sped away.

Frame, who had approached the doorman and his suitcase and was checking it for damage, looked up in alarm when he heard the car pull away.

"But——" said Frame, his hand reaching into his jacket to retrieve his wallet.

The doorman brought a hand up between their faces as he reached with his other hand for the calfskin suitcase.

"God, I hate those guys," he said. He looked at Frame, a smile forming on his handsome sunburned face, showing his movie-star teeth. "No license. Bunch of vultures stealing customers from the licensed crews. They'll get him, one day."

He laughed and with his arm gestured Jameson Frame to the door. "Well, it's your lucky day, I guess. You got yourself a free ride. Welcome to the Hotel des Bains."

SEVEN

∽

An hour later, he at last left his high balcony, lured by the sun and ocean, the sky and the place itself, and the weathered wooden strip of boardwalk, a peripatetic perpetual motion machine of undulating grace and syncopated rhythms.

He made his way through the mid-century lobby of the Hotel des Bains, past the various bars, restaurants and shops, out through what appeared at first to be a seamless gigantic pane of glass, but which opened silently to allow him egress.

He thrashed a bit, blinded by the wall of light that encased him, and blundered past and, to some slight degree, through the outdoor café attached to his hotel, excusing himself to the various and sundry, apologizing for his mad grope of a walk as he wandered down the boardwalk just far enough to reach the first of several large wooden kiosks that sold sunglasses.

Here he tried on a pair or two, somewhat bewildered at the sheer volume of possibilities until he happened to notice a face not far away staring into his own. Regarding the other with a slight tip of his chin, he reached for a pair of aviator lenses in a golden metal frame. The face frowned and shook its head no.

"No?" asked Frame.

"Assuredly, no," the other answered.

Frame ran his fingers over other pairs of lenses, some in ice-blue plastic frames, others in hot pink or acid green.

"Oh, no," she said again—the voice was decidedly female, although it was hard to see the face. "Just wait here."

Frame felt the lack of her presence, although the area was filled with people of all sorts. One group, seemingly a family from the simian way in which they clung to each other, seemed more interested in the pinks, greens and blues than he. He sidled away from them as they descended upon the frames.

Above him, he caught sight of his own face in a small mirror mounted to the kiosk. In the bright sunlight, from what he could make out, he looked a great deal older than he had in the beneficent light of the hotel suite. He pushed his left foot onto tiptoe in order to make out the haze of lines emanating from the corners of his eyes.

"That's why you don't want to buy any cheap sunglasses." The voice again. "Those lines," she said. "They come from squinting in the sun."

"Ah," said Frame, turning his head to face hers.

"Here," she said, handing him an exquisite pair of sunglasses. Lenses with a slight shield shape, tapering ever-so-slightly from top to bottom; their tint, ever-so-slightly darker on the top than on the bottom. The frame was of a burnished metal, light, soft and malleable in his hands.

Frame tried the glasses on and looked at himself again in the mirror. The transformation was astounding. He looked into the glass and saw the image of a rather handsome and certainly successful man looking back at him.

"I knew those would be the ones." As she spoke, the woman moved her face from the left side of Frame's to the right. She gently lifted her hand and touched the corners of the frame, wiggling them slightly to be sure of the fit and then sliding them gently back onto the bridge of his nose. "Perfect," she said.

Frame looked down at the young woman, who, he now could see, was perhaps in her early twenties. She wore a pink ribbon in her brown hair, pink sunglasses of her own, not unlike the cheap pairs that he had surrendered to the family of marauders earlier. When she spoke, he saw that she wore a glossy pink coating on her lips.

"These are excellent," he said. "I'll take them."

"They're not cheap," she warned. "But you get what you pay for. Besides, you look like you could afford them." She smiled.

After paying more than three hundred dollars for the glasses—far more than he had ever expected to pay for a pair of sunglasses, most especially at a beachside wooden kiosk—Frame strolled away from the stand and down the boardwalk. In his light silk suit, his perfectly polished shoes with no socks and his new sunglasses, he felt quite the perfect picture of the prosperous gentleman on a visit.

So, she had assumed by looking at me that I could afford the glasses, Frame thought to himself with a smile on his lips, as he took the case that she had given him, along with a small spray bottle of lens cleaner and a microweave cleaning cloth, and put them in his jacket pocket. *Well why shouldn't she see it*, he thought. *Because I most certainly can.*

There was perhaps something of a saunter in his step as he made his way, dodging the crowd. Reacting to a sudden pang, he stopped and looked at his gloriously expensive watch. He saw the time, craved tea, and yet a voice inside of him suggested that he, just for a moment, stand very still right where he was, with his wrist upraised, so that discerning passersby could note the finery—the suit, the shoes, the belt, the watch, the new, delicious sunglasses and, perhaps, the man who was wearing it all.

Standing there, he noticed at long last the nature of those who swarmed around him. The armada of youths on skateboards, weaving and wending their way through the endless conga of tourists, athletes, drifters, grifters, and preening would-be actors, directors, screenwriters, and just plain movie stars who comprised the village of the boardwalk. In front of him, a muscle cult of sorts had formed on the pipe-metal pull-up bars that were built out and up in concrete, a complete outdoor gym in the sands of the beach, not far from the walkway. Dozens of men, oiled, sweaty or some combination thereof, took turns bouncing pecs and flexing biceps. Some stood to the side, bending one knee to show the bulging calf muscle on the other leg, their arms scooped off to the side, linked at the wrist, like a ballerina's when becoming a swan. All wore Speedos in various colors, although red dominated. These were men with massive musculatures, built over a period of years and tended over like the gardens at Versailles.

Frame watched with some delight, at first as unobtrusively as possible. But then when it became apparent the delight with which these men courted the attention of the crowd, he pulled his new sunglasses down to the tip of his nose in order to get a better look.

Behind and around them, Frame saw the kites in the sky and the young people who ran, often partially naked, underneath them, keeping them aloft. He saw sun worshipers, beach runners, surfers, swimmers, bobbers, and splashers, saw those who picnicked on the sand and those who, from the look of them, had arrived at the beach just in time, so flaccid and pale was their skin.

Frame slipped off his shoes and held them gently by their heels as he walked onto the sand, standing there, experiencing the raucous moment. He stood, sun drenched and heated, exultant, as if in worship of the golden sun above and the sea beyond. The sea that, here, in this place of baubles, colors, shouts, screams, and musical notes, all wafting on the ever-present breeze, all tangled in the kites' tails, was chaste, devoid of color, yet everywhere providing the rhythm rhythm rhythm to which everything responded, from birds' calls to car horns to skates' wheels.

Frame, the pants of his silk suit twisting hard against his legs in the sea breeze, felt himself caught up in it all, a part of this expression of worship of time and place, of moments past and present and yearning for moments that surely will come and then come again. He inhaled deeply, the scent of ocean, salt, sweat, filth, and marijuana all mixed in the air and he raised his arms up over his head in a gesture, an exclamation of joy.

He made his way back to the Hotel des Bains and took a table in the outdoor courtyard. It was after four by then, and the crowd was thinning, so he was able to seat himself quite quickly.

He took a chair at the tiny table that faced the water and waved away the menu, asking for his tea with lemon.

When it arrived, he frowned upon finding that it was already halfway chilled. But he sipped it, marveling again both at the vista in front of him (natural and human) and of the quality of the lenses over his eyes that so completely eliminated all glare.

Sighing and sitting back, he took a moment to study those around him, from the sturdy woman to his right who wore something akin to a muumuu with a large straw hat enveloping her head, to the rather tired couple who passed an exhausted, unconscious child between them. Each would jostle the child a bit, as if to hope to awaken him, and then continue the vacation. The child's head only bobbled, however, and he continued to sleep. "Oh, just give him to me," said the mother, irritated, as the father attempted to hold the sleeping child on the bend of his knee.

She held the child close to her shoulder and the babe glued to her. "Let's just go," she said to her husband, melting into her child as he melted into her. And they paid their bill and were gone.

When they left, Frame noticed a table by the edge of the courtyard, where a young man was sitting, his right foot on a grounded skateboard that his leg moved back and forth, back and forth. He wore wide, loose shorts, a sleeveless T-shirt that betrayed long, lean, well-muscled smooth arms and monstrous athletic shoes that had been frighteningly constructed, no doubt to help keep the boy upright on his board.

Around him were other youths of various ages, who swarmed the seated young man, flying close in and far away. Calling out to him in cawing voices, telling him to *Come, Come on now*. But the youth stayed put, his long smooth left leg stretched out over two chairs, his form recumbent across the edge of the courtyard, as his right held his skateboard in place. Frame allowed his eyes to trail the full length of the man's outstretched leg, from hoof to the hidden upper regions of the crotch. He noted, at the widest point of the calf, that the leg was encircled with the wide band of a tribal tattoo. That Frame could recognize the markings as of Maori origin did not in any way dissipate the sense of horror or the deeper sense of intrigue that the markings gave rise to inside his stomach.

The boy held in his hand the stub end of a hand-rolled cigarette. Frame could smell the scent of it on the wind when the youth exhaled, as if he were exhaling it directly into Frame's lungs. The boy leaned back, extending his neck to the sky and breathed out the last of the smoke.

He noted also another inking of the boy's skin. On the side of the hand, the blunt ridge below the smallest finger, the young man had the image of a multi-faceted diamond tattooed.

Frame studied the perfection of the youth's face, in quarter turns and three quarters, as the shifting of the skateboard caused him to rock in a gentle, undulating motion. He wondered how such a being, in full and apparent possession of his wits, could so mar his body in such a way.

What struck Jameson Frame as so very odd about this vision, aside from the vision itself, perfection of the human form splayed out upon a courtyard not five feet away, was how pale the boy was. How his skin shone white, even waxy, even now in the bright angling of the late afternoon sun.

The youth's friends called to him again, their circles around him growing wider and fuller in indication of their drift.

At last, in one liquid motion, he rose to his feet, stepped over the low wall of the courtyard and onto his board. "Okay," he said, only that. Yet even that startled, as the voice that said even that one small word, was light, high, piping. It was the voice of a boy emanating from the body of a man.

With a twist of his body, an effortless thrust of his being, he moved forward. A hip thrust propelled him off toward the other youths. Just as Frame could begin to comprehend and unravel the markings on the side of the boy's flank that had been seated away from him, the boy gave a single kick of a single foot. And he was gone.

Frame, for lack of a better notion, lifted his cold tea to his lips and tipped the cup. Not enough to allow the cold liquid between his lips, but enough to give that appearance. He was, in fact, transfixed and unsure of what he should do next. Run after the boy? Weep? Or simply return to his room.

"So," said a little voice from behind him. "What did you think of that?"

"What do they all think?" said another voice, a deeper voice, a voice built, year by year, pack by pack, by smoking.

A slight musical note of laughter lifted across the breeze. The gentle little voice spoke again, "He is quite special, our Chase."

"He noticed. Leave him alone."

"Hmmm?" asked Frame, comprehending at last that the two had spoken to him.

"I say, he is quite special, our little Chase?"

"I, ah . . ." said Frame, unsure of the meaning. He turned to the women who sat at the table over his right shoulder. One, a slight older woman with a practical gray bob, twiddled her fingers in his direction.

"I could not help but notice that you, like I, were most entranced by the matinee," said the woman.

"Leave him be now," said the other, much taller woman. She wore what must be a mane of tawny hair up on top of her head, held in place by a large comb of sorts.

"But you forget, Vera, how powerful a vision it is when he is first seen. Like catching sight of an angel." Her hands fluttered like wings. She then turned to Jameson Frame, saying, "How rude of me to comment on your privacy. Let me at least introduce myself, and my dear friend. I am Elsa," she said, providing Frame with an outstretched hand upon which she wore many rings and bracelets. They jangled a simple song as she shook Jameson's hand. "And this is Vera."

"So happy," said Vera, nodding at Frame, without giving explanation as to the source of her pleasure.

"We are so proud of our young thing, you see. Our angel of the seaside, how he flies among us and comes to rest, to visit without visiting."

"Don't worry that you bother him if you stare," said Vera in her low contralto. She coughed a little cough and continued. "I have noticed time and again that, if you stare hard enough, he somehow always seems to feel suddenly quite warm and whips up that shirt of his and exposes his stomach."

"He is very proud of his stomach, Chase is."

"Chase is his name?" asked Frame.

"As far as we know. It is, for him, what passes for a name." Elsa gathered up her straw purse, opened it, found her mirror, and shook her perfectly cut hair. She snapped her purse closed in a simple, clean action, the finality of which suggested that she was preparing to leave.

"Those boys are here every day. Chase usually ends up here in the café. Although he never buys anything, they let him stay. They think he pretties up the place."

"He is there to be looked at, so never worry. He is part of the landscape here, like the sea and the sky. Like Venice itself."

"As are we," said Vera, arising.

"Yes, as are we. We are here much, much too often, mister——?"

"Oh, I'm sorry. Frame. Jameson Frame."

"I hope I may call you, Jameson, as it is such a beautiful name. . . ." said Elsa.

"Please," said Frame. "I hope we shall meet again."

"I am quite sure we shall," said Elsa. "And, in the meantime, enjoy the sights."

Frame arose as the women prepared to leave. He bowed his head in their direction.

Vera paused a moment and spoke conspiratorially. "One thing," she said. "Look long and hard, but take absolutely no photographs unless he gives permission. You see, he is very concerned about what he calls his 'intellectual property.'"

And with Elsa's trill of "goodnight, goodnight," they moved off and out of sight.

EIGHT

ꝏ

The dark entered the room abruptly, after the shimmering glow of the waning sun shifted from persimmon to oxblood. Where Jameson Frame had expected another shade from the color spectrum, something nearer ultraviolet, there was only night.

The many shops, restaurants and clubs that lined the ocean in Venice Beach all were lit brightly, but one had to go to the window, or better, the balcony, to see these, the neon colors, the streetlights, the promises of food, drink, company. But, seen from above, these were just a slight haze of color, no more distinct than the lights on a Christmas tree in the window across the street.

What dominated his view was that thing that could not be seen, that could not be lit: the ocean, which, at night, seemed to torment the place, to place that land on notice that, at any moment, darkness could swallow all light in its cold embrace.

Jameson Frame had dinner from a tray. He ate as he changed the station setting on his television set. He acted, while watching, as if he had never seen such a machine before, as if these sun-dappled local anchors giving the news of the day were something other than he would have seen at home. The night came early now, no matter in which place, and with it, the depressing idea that the light might never come again.

He put his tray in the hall rather than call for service and stretched upward after setting it down. He looked down the long hall to the left, as his was the furthest suite on the right.

He went inside, closing the door silently behind him. He walked through the sitting room of the suite, into the bedroom and on into the bath. There, the sudden glare of the overhead light shocked him out of his dolor, he washed his face with cold water, scrubbed his hands and then stood for a moment taking stock of the room. The tiles, the icy white tiles, so appealing, so cold.

The sheer lack of detail in all the rooms appealed to him, as it stood in direct contrast with his rooms at home.

Tapping the implacable tiles with his fingernails, he turned off the light, went again into the sitting room and watched the television set: real housewives of certain cities, game shows, talk shows, anything, until he could not watch any more.

Just as the food had, the noise of the TV had filled him as well. Set him chattering inside.

He turned off the television, all the lights in the sitting room, and, closing the door, walked into the bedroom and, again, turned off the lights.

Standing there, in mute darkness, Frame felt for the sensation of touch, of his feet against the soft carpet. He stood in the dark, and then, quite suddenly, slipped his hand inside his shirt and ran it, slowly, against his bare skin.

The sudden thrill of it, hand against heartbeat, the back of his hand feeling the soft softness of his immaculate white cotton shirt. The front of it grazing ever so slightly against the soft down of his chest, his nipple, his flank and then the smooth warmth of his belly.

He unbuttoned the shirt with his other hand, as he needed to let skin smooth along skin.

Looking out through the large uncovered window into the darkness beyond, he pulled the shirt from the pants and dropped it, not bothering to notice as it fell. He unbuckled his pants and allowed them to fall, too, stepped out of them and of his white cotton boxers.

He walked quietly to the balcony door, opened it, and stepped out, completely nude. Jameson Frame felt the light rush of the night wind against his skin. Saw lights below, far, far below and darkness ahead and all around. He heard and smelled the ocean. He welcomed it with arms that he briefly outstretched and then pulled back, placing them first on his head and then letting them wilt down to his sides.

He walked past the table at the edge of the balcony and stood there, his toes slipping underneath the raised short glass wall, tickling the spot where the frame of the glass met the supportive metal.

Here, Frame felt a peace that had been quite impossible in his room. Now he was surrounded by the light and noise of this everyday evening. Here, with the moonless darkness, the very few, brave stars that managed to shine in spite of all else that was here going on, the haze of the village below, the constant rhythmical sound of the ocean itself, there was, in Jameson Frame, a building sensation of quiet and contentment.

In a moment, after feasting upon his own emotions, he sat, rather spent, upon the cold metal of the café chair on the balcony. Felt the rounded, bas-relief of the thing against his ass, his balls, and leaned back, luxuriating in the cool hardness of it. In feeling so exposed to the intemperate experience of the chair, the open air of the balcony and beyond— that great undefinable darkness of beyond—Frame felt something rise in his throat, a cough, perhaps, or a whimper, or a whisper of surrender. For it seemed, quite suddenly, as if he were a child who was afraid of the dark.

His nights at home were things accounted for. With work and deadlines and set times for dinner, contemplation, sleep. But here, now, night was when things slipped in or slipped away. With the sound of the ocean, in its ongoing assault upon the shore. Facing it, hearing it, smelling it, but unable to see it, to touch it, Frame found himself so vulnerable to it all.

He could have ended it in a second. Flipping on a switch. Putting on his soft white robe. Dressing and going out to visit with the multitude that was, even now, dancing, eating, farting, laughing, touching.

And yet, he sat, nude, cold, more than a little frightened, at his little café table on the balcony, listening to the sound of the sea.

Later, the door of the balcony was still wide open, the sound of the sea the only thing to be heard in the quiet room, the town at last quiet down below, Jameson Frame lay on his bed, the impossibly smooth cotton of the sheets slick against his nude body. He had pulled the top sheet across his groin, allowing his legs to remain uncovered, as was his chest, his head, his neck and his arms.

He lay, arms at his sides, in the semblance of quietude, as the night pressed hard against his closed eyes.

His breathing was shallow. His heart danced in his chest. He felt a presence in the room with him. An energy that, when it filled the room and touched him, first on the flat of his right foot and the pointed toes of the left and then upward, swallowing him, as if the ocean were filling the room, lifted him slightly, so that he felt himself floating within the warm pulsation of energy.

The energy rose in his body. It traveled up his legs, until it tickled his testes. As it caressed his penis, he felt it rise into a full erection. The energy filled his body, filled the room, lifting him upward, many inches off the bed.

Unafraid, he allowed himself to lift his arms within it. Felt it lightly sweep the hairs on his body, while the night still pressed full upon his closed eyes. Even with them held tight, he could sense the slightest tinge of red in the room, a gentle light that suffused the force. He arched his back within it, delighting in his weightlessness and in the sheer sense of potency that he felt.

As if young. He heard within himself.

"Yes. As if young."

Carefully, he opened his eyes, just a slit at first, and then more fully, until his eyes were opened and accustomed to the dim red light.

And he looked at his own hands and saw the markings. He saw on his arms and legs, on his torso as well, the markings, the Maori markings, covering his hide in full. And heard, within the ocean's rush, the beating of the drums.

Jameson Frame woke with a start, his body cold, uncovered. He gathered the sheet, and pulled at the blanket below it, making, as best he could without fully waking himself, a nest of warmth and comfort. He pulled himself into a fetal position within his nest, drawing his legs up and his arms in. In one swirling motion, he brought the soft sheets up over his head and allowed them to flutter down again, drowning him in the comfort.

And he slept. He slept at last, long and hard, until the light of morning penetrated the room.

When he awakened, far later than he would have believed possible with doors open and windows uncovered, Jameson Frame checked his own smooth body as thoroughly as possible and scrubbed it carefully in a hot bath.

Jameson Frame then had oatmeal for breakfast. With raisins and honey and a little cinnamon. He ate on his balcony, dressed in his soft soft white robe. And when the shafts of sunlight began their march around the corners of the building, making mirrors of all reflective surfaces, the spoons, the tea, Frame put on his sunglasses and studied the day. As he lounged, a long leg reaching out in front of him, pointing toward the sea, he looked every bit a man in his moment—in the place and time of his own selecting.

As always, when he ate, he ate slowly and then arose to dress and venture out to discover the pleasures of the day.

NINE

The important thing, from what he was given to understand, was that the card was upside down. Inverted, to use the appropriate jargon. The whole meaning given the card was because the man pictured on it was not hanging, as the card drew him, but was, instead, standing on one outstretched foot, with the other foot bent behind him, knee far out, like a Russian dancer about to leap. The foot of the leg with the bent knee was passed behind the straightened leg and pointed out behind him. The man's hair, which would have looked as if gravity were pulling the long mass of it downward had the card been upright, stood up off his head now. Like snakes perhaps—Medusa wearing a writhing pompadour. Or like tongues of fire emanating from the man's skull. Around the whole of the man's head was a nimbus of light, perhaps attaching a meaning of holiness to the image.

The man's arms were bent with elbows jutted both outward and upward, his arms at his hips, his palms at the small of the back. He wore the simple clothing of a peasant, a jerkin and tights.

Jameson Frame looked down at the card each time a fingernail tapped it and looked up again into Vera's eyes each time she began to explain. He bent his head in closer, as if he were hard of hearing, straining to comprehend what this card might possibly have to do with him.

When he'd come down from his breakfast that morning, dressed as if for Bermuda in wide cotton shorts, a lightweight white shirt and a blue blazer, Elsa had hurried to him and taken him by the hand. "We waited for you and hoped you would take coffee with us," she said as she led him back to the outdoor café. "Such a lovely morning, don't you think?"

"Indeed," said Jameson Frame, who, before sitting, apologized to the women for not having taken care to properly introduce himself when they met the day before.

"Thank you, Mr. Frame," said Elsa. "It is so good to know you."

"And good morning to you both, Elsa and Vera," said Frame, nodding to each as he mentioned their names.

He studied the menu for a moment as if he were still hungry. When the waiter came he ordered coffee and, thinking of the women, a platter of sliced fruit, looking at each of them for approval as he spoke.

"Ah, Mr. Frame," Elsa began.

"Please. Jameson," he said.

"Jameson. Ah, good. Yes. I wanted to tell you that our friend Vera has a gift. She is something of a psychic and yesterday, when she met you, she said to me after, 'Elsa, I must read that man. I am quite certain that our meeting was in no way accidental.' Vera felt strongly that we would be running into you this morning, so she brought along her cards. Would you be so kind as to let Vera read for you?"

Vera pulled a packet of large cards wrapped in a large silk scarf out of her purse and held them out to Jameson with a quizzical look. He nodded, and she quickly began to spread the cards out on the table and shuffle them. She slapped them down in front of Jameson.

"Cut," she said. And Frame cut the cards.

She gathered them up and laid the cards out in a pattern.

In the center was the card named The Hanged Man, in reverse.

"This is the card that represents you, Jameson. So it's an important card. Pay attention."

She tapped the card with her indigo violet fingernail and looked at him from behind the gigantic dark glasses, dark gray lenses in a black frame. He tried to see her eyes, but could not, could only ascertain movement behind the lenses. The wind gently teased her already teased yellow hair.

Jameson's attention briefly drifted with the breeze.

"You must pay attention, Jameson," said Elsa in a tinkling voice, coating her admonition with honey.

Vera again tapped the card.

"This is a card that is itself something of a riddle. When the card is upright, you see, the image is upside down. And when the card inverts, the image rightens. For this alone, it is the only card in the deck that follows such a pattern. So, we begin with an enigma of sorts, a man, like the card, who does not fit the usual pattern."

The waiter appeared with the food and Jameson's coffee. He began to put the tray in the center of the tiny table, but saw the spread of cards and paused.

"Could we have that here?" asked Jameson, indicating the small table to his side upon which he was resting his elbow. The waiter sidestepped the company and placed the food on the adjoining table. Thanked, he moved on without a backward glance.

"So we're not like other people, are we, Jameson? Quite out of the ordinary. But we had guessed that. That we knew.

"None of those fanny packs for you, Jameson, eh?"

"Vera and I were saying just last night how very wonderful we thought you were, how mannerly," said Elsa, who was taking from her purse a packet of long, thin cigarettes.

Noticing that Jameson noticed her intent, she asked, "Does anyone mind if I smoke outdoors? I find smoking quite thrilling in the open air." As no one minded, she lit her cigarette before Jameson could reach over to assist her. "No more interruptions, Vera," she said. "Begin again."

"But he had heard that already," said Vera.

"More important to move on."

"The Hanging Man, if he is indeed hanging, as he should be, is a card that indicates great change," Vera continued. "You see the man in this card appears on another card as well. He is called The Fool. And by this I mean that he is an innocent, Jameson, and not in any way indicating that you are foolish. Indeed, you have a deep abhorrence of foolishness. This Fool seeks new adventures, perhaps a whole new way of life. He feels unsatisfied with his life, particularly with his work. He feels unfulfilled, and as if he can never, in the time left, manage to create something fine enough, or wise enough to last. Do you follow me, Jameson?"

Jameson Frame realized that he was sitting bolt upright in his chair. He nodded as Vera again tapped the card with her fingernail.

"Now The Fool goes and sits under this tree for eight days. He just waits, absorbing everything around him, learning from everyone. On the ninth day he takes action and climbs the tree and hangs from it. So The Hanging Man is not, in the most real sense of the word, hanged. He is not being put to death, but is himself hanging from the tree of his own free will. Because this image has a great deal to do with free will. Nothing is being forced on The Hanging Man. All is by his own choice.

"Now the riddle of the card is not just the why of it—why hang there? But also, how long can he last, hanging there? The first part can be answered by noting that, in climbing and hanging, he is totally changing his perspective. Seeing and experiencing things in a new way.

"But the second part—who can say how long he can last before he must take action and make definitive changes? The man is in need of a new direction in life, a new way of seeing and doing, and yet he continues to hang there, with all his might, until he can hang no more.

"Now, invert the image again, Jameson, turn the card so that you see it upside down. The switch from upright to upside down causes the meaning to change as well. Not the whole meaning. The major ideas are the same. The waiting. The hanging on with all one's might when change is needed. The need for action to root out rootlessness and the feeling of being incomplete or not having done all one could have."

She traced around the form of the man with the edge of her finger-nail. "See him, Jameson? Beware of him. When he moves upside down a certain selfishness begins to grow. And his sacrifice, unless he is very, very careful, is for nothing. Upright, this is a sacred card, a sacred process. Upside down, profane."

Without asking, Vera reached for Elsa's slim cigarette and puffed on it. With it still between her lips, she said, "So. An interesting vacation you are having, Jameson."

"Indeed," he said quietly.

"Oh, dear," said Elsa. "Put the cards away, I don't think he could stand to hear any more about them."

Jameson watched as Vera gathered her cards into a silk scarf and bound the cards tight by tying the edges. She dropped the cards back into Elsa's purse and took a long, hard drag on the cigarette before stubbing the butt out on the metal tabletop.

For a moment, Jameson found himself preparing to leave. He pulled the tray of food over to the table in front of them and cleared his throat. Elsa placed her butterfly of a hand on the edge of his sleeve, pulling him quite gently back into the chair and the conversation.

"Mr. Frame," she said, "Jameson. Are you here in our little village to work? Is there some new poetry collection or perhaps a novel?"

"I had come here for a change of view," he said, and Vera looked at Elsa and tapped the tabletop with the tip of her fingernail. "But, now that I am here, I find myself thinking about writing."

"Oh, how very exciting," said Elsa. "And, of course, we know who you are. I must confess that, when we went home last night we Googled you."

Not sure exactly what that entailed, Jameson managed only an "Ah," as he nodded his head. "I'll just have to find a way to arrange for a typewriter."

"A typewriter?" asked Vera. "Why not use a laptop like everyone else? Make some changes. Move with us into the new millennium, Jameson." She twisted the large diamond ring on her finger.

"You are a most impressive man, Mr. Frame," said Elsa. "One who deserves to have the finest tools of his craft. It is hard to believe that one who can produce such work as *On Scrimshaw and Others* is relying on a mere typewriter, when the computer can allow you to do ever so much more."

She lifted a slice of watermelon to her lips. The corners of her mouth raised themselves in a vague smile. She took a bite.

"Go look at them, at least. You will be amazed at how beautiful they are. If you like, we can accompany you and show you the type we ourselves purchased not long ago. The shop is not far from here. Besides it would be very good to step away from this hotel."

"I guess," said Jameson Frame lightly, "there is no harm in looking." And he nudged the plate of fruit toward the women, who each happily accepted a strawberry.

Not long later, Jameson Frame sat in his suite, his navy coat neatly hung over the chair by the desk. On top of the desk was his slim gleaming purchase, a pale shade of aluminum perhaps, or, better still, platinum. All around were various boxes, but in front of him was only the computer and the slimmest and smallest of printers that would print both silently and wirelessly. The hotel had sent a boy to hook the thing up and to load the machine with what software it needed. Now, ready, fully invested with everything required for recording his every thought, it hummed before him.

He flipped open the lid as he had been shown. The keyboard suddenly glowed with life. He awakened the word processing software as taught and, when the blank white void appeared before him, as blank as any paper could ever be, he put his hands to the keys and typed—marveling at the touch of the keys, their soft bounce—words so reminiscent of Ruskin: "The Waters of Venice," before adding, "California."

Jameson Frame spent what turned out to be the better part of three hours working on his computer, opening and closing various software mostly, and pondering the nature of what he hoped would become a rather fine prose poem on the sea as it rumbaed out before him. From his desk, which faced a window in the sitting room overlooking the Pacific, Frame found new inspiration with every glance. The sea itself was his muse.

The women (or "those women" as Frame tended to consider them in the privacy of his own thoughts) had told him that they would meet him later on the beach itself, as they had a yen to lie in the sand. He had agreed to this before having experienced working with his new tool. "Still," he thought, arising from his chair and stretching his back by pressing both his palms against it and leaning side to side.

"Oh, well," he said to himself as he snapped the computer shut. And "Oh, shit," he said quite loudly as he ran back to make quite sure he had saved the document on which he had been working.

When he left, he purposely left his navy coat behind, wearing only his Bermuda shorts and white shirt, with his sockless slip-ons on his feet. He reached for his sunglasses as he neared the door, and put his room key in his pocket. Looking briefly at his reflection in the mirror next to the door, he noted that, without his knowledge or permission, the California sun had already changed his complexion from tapioca to *café con leche*. And he found himself appreciating the change.

TEN

❦

$\mathbf{A}$s he left the protective zone of the hotel and its courtyard café, Jameson Frame felt himself immediately vulnerable. Instantly, as he stepped from under the hotel façade onto the boardwalk, he was swallowed within the conga line of general merriment that was the everyday foot traffic of the place. As he had watched it from above, it had appeared as layers of movement, skaters and bicyclists wending in among people walking, people dancing, people buying and selling, and people living there in that narrow stretch of land.

Layers within layers within layers, each, from above, seemed distinct, but here, looking at it head on, living within it, the mass seemed a solid whole, made up of disparate parts. The skaters seemed to want nothing to do with the rest of the multitude. They congregated in a park that had apparently been created for them all out of concrete, a large rectangle of hills, valleys, steps, and ramps. The skaters careened from all directions and, as they assembled, there seemed something of a pecking order that established who might skate and when. Those newly arriving sat at the edge of the park, closely watching the action within. From time to time, there was a shrill call of horror followed by either laughter or applause. From time to time, the injured picked up their fractured skateboards and walked to the far edge of the crowd; from there they leaned in to watch with the others. Or, seated faced away from the action, rolled fat cigarettes and smoked them, arching their backs to look hard into the sky and laughing and nudging others more or less continually.

Those on bicycles had a path of their own, carved between the boardwalk and the sand. This barrier, with bicycles coming from both directions at what seemed like automotive speeds, proved daunting to Jameson

Frame, who more than once considered either returning to his suite or buying a taco from a nearby stand instead of attempting to get past them.

While he stood, rocking his weight from his left foot to his right, he thought he heard his name called. Looking up and over, he saw Elsa, with her enormous white-framed sunglasses in one hand, waving to him with a long silk scarf that she held in the other.

Emboldened, he hurried across the bicycle path and onto the sand.

Until that moment, he had wondered why, when he looked out his window, he often saw that the sand was all but deserted. This wide patch of sand, the pathway to the sea. He had expected, before arriving here, that the beach would be the hub of social life. And yet, it was not, the boardwalk, with its many kiosks, shakes and handcarts, was where the people gathered.

"Why, the sand is filthy!" exclaimed Jameson Frame as he looked down at the detritus that could be seen mixed in with the heavy damp sand.

"Look out for needles," said Vera.

"Yes, it can be disappointing," said Elsa as she walked over and took Frame's hand, leading him to their encampment. "But, as you see, we brought with us a tiny hoe, so as to create the perfect Japanese garden in which to sit," she said, gesturing him into a strangely colored tent. "You must visit our sukkah. We brought with us some rugs and some batik fabric for the walls. The lovely men gave up some of their exercise time to tie together sticks for us, as they so often will do."

The resultant structure, built open to the ocean waves, was remarkably luxurious, with comfortable folding chairs, a small folding table and a picnic basket tucked into the rear of the tent. Someone—Elsa, no doubt—had strung to the front a strange mobile of sorts, one in which a copperish Moroccan diamond-patterned shape contained a slightly smaller identical piece and so forth and so forth, so that, when the wind blew, the object seemed a thing alive, pulsing with interior movement. It fascinated him, hypnotized him, as it moved in conjunction with the wind and waves.

"Pretty thing, huh?" asked Vera.

"Yes," he answered.

His attention drawn back from the mobile, he realized for the first time that Elsa herself was akin to her structure. She wore a loose garment made from the same batik pattern as the wall beside her. Each puckered and pulsated with the wind. Around her neck was a strand of wooden beads so large that, had they been carved from stone, the weight of them would have rendered her unable to lift her head. In her short hair, she had a beaded headband, into which a small yellow flower was poked. She had placed her sunglasses on the top of her head, and, seeing her face closely for the first time, Frame was taken aback to see how apparently young she was, her face smooth, her skin perfect and unblemished and luminously white, as if it had never seen the sun.

"You must have that when we are done here," said Elsa. "The little wind toy," she continued, nodding toward it. "You must hang it up in your room tonight to enjoy the motion there."

"How nice," said Jameson Frame and "thank you," before Vera, reaching up to him with surprisingly large hands, pulled him rather roughly into a chair. He settled in with something like a sigh, and watched the surfers who, like the skaters on land, seemed to have a secret means of selection by which they as a group always knew whose turn it was to ride the waves next.

As he watched, Elsa went into the picnic chest, and withdrew a bottle. Frame heard the sudden pop of it and turned just as Elsa asked, "Would you care for a glass of some really rather fine champagne?"

All through a cold meal consisting of crabmeat and various cheeses, all served on exotic crackers of the sort that Frame had never seen before, he felt Vera's eyes on him. At last she spoke.

"I hope you don't mind, Mr. Frame, if Elsa and I make a bit of a project out of you."

"Eh?" managed Frame.

"We spoke about it last night, Mr. Frame——" said Vera.

"We spoke of how we wished that your vacation with us here would be the finest of your life, Jameson, and how we wished we could make sure that it would be," said Elsa, with a sweet, unwrinkled smile. "Would that be all right with you?"

Feeling in that moment, in that place, the batik sukkah placed in exactly the right place to give him the best experience possible of the waves, the gulls and the surfers, champagne in one hand, a slice of fruit in the other, quite cared for, he heard himself agree.

"For example, Jameson," Elsa said conspiratorially, moving a bit closer to him, "Have you ever considered . . ." Her hands danced in the air, came close to his face. Suddenly her palms flattened. "But no. Never mind."

"Have I considered what, Elsa?"

"Oh, some nonsense of mine. Not to be remembered or brought up again . . ."

"I may well have considered it," he said. "I have, in my time, considered a good many things."

She laughed a laugh of tiny bell sounds. "I just have noticed that when you smile your beautiful smile, Jameson, that all around your eyes, all around here," and she brushed the edge of her hand lightly against the skin below and next to his eyes, "shows a good deal of age. I had wondered if you had ever considered doing something about it."

"Doing what?"

"I myself see a wonderful man who keeps my skin rather nice." And she displayed her skin to Jameson, tipping her cheek toward him, her own hand framing the edge of her face.

"Rather nice?" demanded Vera. "Not since Luciana Pignatelli has there been skin like that. Not since Grace Kelly. Had she lived, seeing skin like this on someone else would have killed her."

"Yes, I see," said Jameson Frame. "But—"

"It is only that you are such an attractive man, Jameson, and that you are so much in the public eye. I should so like to introduce you to the man who is of such help to me so that you can show yourself with full dignity and valor."

More than he would have admitted, Jameson Frame was intrigued with the twin notions of dignity and valor.

"I don't see why I can't at least meet the man," said Frame, at which Elsa clapped her hands lightly. She then reached across for Frame's hand, and as he bent his body toward her, she took the hand gently into her light grip, lowered her lips and lightly kissed it.

Vera, who had just finished off a rather large glass of champagne, took the opportunity with Frame drawn near to slip her index finger into the inside of his shirt collar. She pulled him close in her direction, looked down his shirt and exclaimed, "I cannot quite believe the amount of chest hair down there!"

Frame, his face reddening, leaned back in his chair.

He was sure that as he did so he heard Elsa murmur, "Oh, dear," but was quite unclear as to her meaning.

"And look at the legs!" Vera exclaimed, not quite finished, "Good Lord, a pelt!"

At which point, Elsa looked up into Frame's eyes.

"What do you think about a stroll up the promenade, Jameson?" she asked. "Perhaps we should allow Vera to have the opportunity of some quiet for an afternoon nap?"

Jameson Frame watched from a bit of a distance as the women took down the chairs and laid them aside. Elsa then helped Vera to lie down on the rug, and rolled the tablecloth for her as she pulled herself further into the tent and placed her back against both the view and the rising afternoon winds, winds that had only minutes before changed their direction as they did every afternoon, so that they were now coming in from the ocean and quickly cooling the land. Elsa gently touched Vera's long, thick yellow hair as a benediction of sort, brought her fingers to her lips and kissed them, then slowly dropped her fingers as if to scatter the kisses over her friend.

She walked over to Frame and slipped her arm in his. As they approached the bicycle lane, all traffic seemed to suddenly stop, allowing them easy passage. In the same way, the skaters, the walkers, the tourists, and the homeless all seemed quite willing to give them room, not only to walk but to walk abreast. Whereas, earlier, he had been jostled, poked, and threatened while trying to make his way down to the beach.

As it had when he first laid his ogling eyes on the place just scant days ago, the boardwalk reminded him of nothing so much as a Bedouin market, one that, despite the size of it and the churning energy all around, might well fold up at any time and move on. The fact that, as one walked, one saw, in the distance, large white buildings, important looking structures with a fixed locale and a strict point of view, only served to enhance the transient feel of the place, as did the various beads and sandals worn by its inhabitants, and by their beards and long hair.

It was a place of rubble, it seemed to him, a place born from rubble and to rubble to return.

Where most Californians feared the potential earthquake, those living in Venice needed only to fear a strong wind, as that would be all that it would take to blow the rickety place down. A good storm could eradicate Venice once and for all and clean the sands of its memory, dirty needles included.

Still, Elsa seemed quite joyful as she walked along. She gave his arm a tender squeeze when she saw him look her way.

And these others, these overweight tourists with cameras built into everything—phones, belt buckles, hats, what have you—seemed to be grinning as well, as did the stoned youth and the middle-aged folks who seemed to have sold them the pot.

It was as if there was something in the air.

Frame himself laughed aloud after thinking this, feeling as if he were finally in on the joke. Something in the air. Indeed.

Within the brief period of their stroll, Elsa and Jameson played foosball in an arcade and drank frozen lemonade as they walked. Jameson helped Elsa select a large, floppy woven hat in order to keep her face out of the sun, as she had left her picture hat in the tent on the beach. He insisted that she allow him to buy it for her when she realized that she had also left her purse with Vera.

"It is nothing. Less than nothing. It is a joy to have something to give to you," he said as she placed it on her head, her features disappearing under it.

When they had turned and were once again approaching the Hotel des Bains, Elsa asked, "And do you eat nightshades?"

"Pardon?" asked Jameson Frame, genuinely confused.

"Nightshades. Do you eat them—eggplants, peppers, tomatoes and such?"

"Oh. Yes. Certainly."

"I am so glad," she said, squeezing his arm once more. "Vera and I had hoped that we could occupy your time again this evening. We don't wish to monopolize you, but we have made enough stuffed eggplant for an army, you see, and we are having some friends around. We had hope we could include you and introduce you to some locals."

Before he could answer, she added, "Besides, you have yet to see our canals."

"I should be very happy to," he answered, and she gave him a little card that was embossed with her first name and Vera's, intertwined, with an address below.

"I'm so pleased," she said. "May we say eight tonight? That gives you time to rest and change for what I hope will be a very pleasant evening."

Soon after, as Jameson Frame walked past the mess of electronics boxes and over to the window in his suite, he watched Vera and Elsa emerge from their sukkah, picnic basket in hand, while several men rushed over from the nearby outdoor gym. Their bodies glistened in the waning sun as each kissed Vera and then Elsa, and, as the women walked away arm in arm, Vera swinging the basket on her free arm, the men made short work of dismantling the structure and carting it away.

ELEVEN

∽

Alighting from the taxi some hours later, Jameson Frame took stock of what he saw.

To his left, as he paid the driver, was what must have been what stood in for a canal. To his eyes, it was a culvert of sorts. Something that had been meant to suggest a canal, perhaps, but, even at night could not be mistaken for one.

It was, as Frame knew it would be, a fake. But, like so many of the fakes he had encountered here, it was, perhaps, prettier than the real, if not vaguely transitory. With Japanese bridges, box hedges and red row-boats floating in clear water, tied to the hedges with a single gold cord, it suggested Hollywood more than Venice.

He poked along the edges of the waterway for as long as he thought he might. Not only because he enjoyed the sight of what passed for a dark water mystery in this sun-drenched place, but also because he was not sure that he altogether wished to enter the house that now stood to his rear.

When the taxi (which he had not really needed—the distance was slight enough, had he had more confidence in his ability to find the place or to arrive safely after dark) first pulled up, Frame had been taken aback to hear the sound of loud music and by the movement of what appeared to be many people that he could see through the windows of the small white cottage.

Nevertheless, having done everything that he might to enjoy the waterway, short of taking out a coin and tossing it in with a wish and a prayer, he crossed the tiny road, slipped between the bumpers of two tightly parked cars, and pushed open the little white gate in the picket fence.

Just inside the fence was a garden of scents: lavender, sage, old tea roses, and high butterfly bushes. Rising from the center of the lawn was a small Japanese maple, under which a small, very rickety looking bench had been placed. Beyond the tree, almost hidden by it, was a small white cottage.

It was as if the cottage once had been a family-sized house and then shrunken, miniaturized by a third, so that everything, the gate, the yard, the porch, and the house itself, was all rather tenderly reduced to the point of being almost too small for human habitation.

Almost. And yet, here it was, with two small chairs on the porch, one of which had an old, tattered pillow lying across the seat. The pillow sagged in the middle to suggest years of wear.

Jameson Frame stood, dressed again in his fine silk suit, with one foot on the single step up to the porch, his attention lost on the wild clumps of bleeding hearts that grew from boxes and cascaded over the edge of the porch. Someone, it seemed to him, had rather lovingly watered these just as the sun faded opalescent on the horizon. This, for some reason, seemed terribly meaningful to him.

"Jameson?"

He looked up. Elsa stood in a long flowing version of the batik dress that she wore that afternoon. He could see the outline of her body through the sheer fabric. She was barefoot. She held the screen door open, beckoning him inside.

"Jameson, come in. We were waiting for you."

He approached her as she opened the door wide. "You have such a lovely yard," he said, "that I got quite caught up."

"How very nice, Jameson. Welcome," she said to him, as she craned her neck upward and kissed him softly on his lips. Her kiss, like her touch, was like butterfly wings alighting softly, briefly. She smelled like the lavender in her garden.

"Hello, everyone," Elsa said in a voice that was lost over the sound of the ancient stereo in the back of the room. But perhaps because they were used to the sound of her voice, most of the others looked up. In the back of the room, right next to the stereo itself, Jameson Frame caught sight of Vera dancing a slow cha cha with a very tall, dignified woman who would later be introduced to him only as "Frau Schmidt."

Vera, sensing Elsa's words, lifted the needle off the record. The impact was tremendous. Elsa's little singsong voice suddenly sounded very loud.

"My dears, this is our new friend, Mr. Jameson Frame, the well-known man of letters who has left dreary New York behind to spend some time with us here. I hope you will greet him, because I know you will soon be as fond of him as Vera and I are."

Soon, Jameson had been welcomed over onto the long low, very aged couch, where he sat in some discomfort between Kiki, who appeared to most likely be a young, slender man dressed as a sort of chanteuse, with a blond wig made from some sort of polyester material sitting ever so slightly askew on his head, and a very large exotic gentleman named Bobo, who had promised Vera that he would, later in the evening, entertain everyone by playing his drum. Seated on the coffee table facing him, with his knees intertwined with Frame's was Kiki's friend, who, in passing, seemed to have introduced himself to Jameson Frame as "Smack."

It was his presence that Frame found to be particularly oppressive, both because of the smells that were coming off of him and because he seemed to quite often wish to favor Frame with a little friendly pressure from his bare knees. Bend though he might, Frame seemed quite incapable of escape until a large yellow cat chose to jump into his lap.

Startled, Frame let out a bit of a yelp, to the entertainment of those around him. From the edge of the room, he heard Vera growl, "Oh, that damned cat!" while Elsa hurried over to apologetically lift him from Frame's lap.

Jameson Frame took this opportunity to lift himself off the couch—no easy task in that it, like the rest of the furniture in the place, seemed to be sagging with age, something that Elsa no doubt had sought to make up for by scattering layers upon layers of pillows everywhere, the dense softness of which made it difficult for Frame to pull himself up and onto his feet.

With a sudden assistance from Smack, who leaped to his feet, pulled Frame to his and then replaced him and sat next to Kiki on the couch, Frame found himself free and able to maneuver around the crowded little room.

The screen door swung shut behind Elsa who, having put the cat out for the night, apologized repeatedly. Jameson Frame smiled and waved and nodded to her, thanked her for removing the cat and moved on to explore the rear of the home.

He walked past the doorway to the dining room which held an old, very large picnic table with two long benches and several mismatched seats, and entered the kitchen just in time to walk directly into someone who had just entered through the back door.

Apologizing and stepping back, Frame recognized the beautiful young man whom he had seen the day before—could it be so short a space of time?—at his hotel's outdoor café. The skateboarder with the Maori tattoo.

Frame excused himself once more. Looking directly into the young man's nighttime eyes. Watching as the corners of those eyes wrinkled into a bright smile that his mouth soon mirrored. All the boy's emotions, Frame noticed, seemed to begin in his eyes.

"I am so sorry," said Frame. "So clumsy of me . . ."

"Hey, no problem, man."

The youth showed no signs of recognition and displayed no need to move on. He stood, rather vacantly, as if waiting for Frame to say something more. As he had the day before, he wore only overlarge shorts and a sleeveless low-cut pullover that displayed his muscled arms to their best effect.

Before Frame could say another word, they heard Vera's voice and each turned to see her standing in the kitchen doorway.

"Oh, you two found each other? Good," said Vera. "Elsa! Chase is here."

Elsa hurried from whatever conversation she had been having to join Vera in the doorway of the kitchen.

"Oh, I did so want the two of you to have the chance to get to know each other," said Elsa, with a broad cat smile on her face. "I gave this little party hoping that you could become acquainted." It seemed to Frame that Elsa's words had special meaning targeted at him and that her smile carried a heavy message.

"Chase, this is Jameson Frame. He is a very important and influential writer from New York City and a very good new friend of ours. I hope you will tell him all about yourself. He may want to write a book about you," she said with a wink.

The boy snorted and gave Frame what could only have been described—were he indeed writing the book about the boy—as an enticing grin. The boy's snort indicated perhaps pleasure, but, notably, not disbelief.

"Jameson, Chase here is one of our treasures. He is quite the special boy, so skilled in so many things. I know you will have much to talk about and will become great friends."

Suddenly, a figure emerged from the darkness and pressed itself hard against the outside of the kitchen screen door.

"Hey, where are you?"

"That's just my brother. Mikey," said the youth. "I came in to get us some beer."

Vera went to the refrigerator and pulled out two cans of cold beer. She threw them to the boy. "Dinner's in about twenty minutes," she said, "so don't go far."

The youth caught the cans and pulled them against his chest as he pushed against the door, shoving his brother out into darkness.

"We'll be right back," he said, before pointing his chin in Jameson's direction and adding, "Good to meet you, man. Later?"

"Later," answered Jameson, again almost as a question. His face reddened in the kitchen's glaring overhead light, as he thought of the boy, and pondered the internal engine that drove him to speak such a word as "later."

TWELVE

࿚

The better part of an hour later, Oscar Peterson's *Pastel Moods* playing on the stereo with the occasional scratch creating a jump in the music, which repeated again and again thanks to the stereo's upraised arm, most of the guests were seated around the picnic table, with paper plates mounded with sections of stuffed eggplant that had turned chocolate brown in baking and a yellow aromatic covered in pumpkin seeds.

Jameson Frame picked at the food on his plate with the white plastic fork he had been provided, along with a steak knife and an iced-tea spoon. Paper towels served as napkins. Frame had managed to get himself a seat on the far end of the table facing both the living room doorway and the front door by being polite enough to say, "Oh, no, after you," to all comers until the rest of the bench had been filled. Thus, it was only Kiki beside him to his right and Elsa who sat across the table from him who were his dinner companions. From Kiki, he learned that the music scene in Venice was below that of other, less colorful parts of the greater Los Angeles area, unless one wanted to be a part of a drum circle (whatever that was. Frame decided, when it was mentioned, not to ask, but nodded instead).

Elsa regularly got up from her seat and went into the kitchen, where she first opened the oven, took the aluminum-foil wrapping from the top of the remaining eggplant and pressed on it with her fingertip. She then put the foil back on the food, tenting it, and, closing the oven door, she tenderly adjusted the temperature dial. She went to the kitchen door, time after time, and looked out into the darkness beyond, standing very still, in the apparent hope that she would be able to hear what she could not see, over the mixed sounds of the conversation, sporadic laughter and the melted chocolate sounds of jazz.

Each time, Frame watched as Elsa adjusted her face from a private frown to the smile that she presented to her assembled guests.

In the intervening time since he himself stood in the kitchen, unable to breathe in the presence of the beautiful youth, Jameson Frame had divested himself of his suit jacket, which he slid oh, so, carefully onto the back of the couch, folding it lovingly. He had made something of a show of this, in that he had hoped that he would be offered a hanger and a place in a closet somewhere by one of his hostesses, both of whom watched him fold his coat gently and offered him only a smile and a nod.

He made sure that he transferred his wallet from the coat to his pants pocket.

And, in a spirit of bonhomie, he slipped his shoes off as well, placed them under the end of the couch and dug his toes into the cabin's ancient pile carpeting.

He sat now, wishing that he could lean back on this ridiculous bench. And wishing as well that Chase, the beautiful youth, would come back into the party, with his brother or without.

Chase. He mouthed the word while chewing a mouthful of fragrant rice. He had decided, upon tasting the eggplant, that he was indeed adverse to deadly nightshades.

In that moment, as if conjured in a miraculous wish fulfillment, Chase and his brother entered through the back door, slamming it, and walked into the room, laughing. They sat at the far end of the table in two mismatched chairs by the kitchen door, the brother in a plastic folding chair and Chase, as if he were host and lord of the manner, in the sole plush cushioned one.

He sat back into the pillowed comfort of the chair, crossing his palms behind his head, exposing his armpits and their thick, black hair to all assembled and displaying a nearly life-sized tattoo of a skateboard with the word "California" written on it that ran the length of the underside of his arm.

The youth sat with his eyes half closed, perhaps listening to the music that wafted around the room, perhaps allowing the bright lights and the general chatter to rain over his consciousness. His face seemed impossibly erotic as he leaned in half shadow, his arms and legs bare, his body barely contained in the clothes that covered it.

Elsa, as the boys came into the room, ran into the kitchen to pile food on two more plates. She brought them in and placed them in front of the boys, offering them either more of the beer that they had had earlier or some of the wine that the rest were drinking from cups, bowls and glasses of various sorts. The brother, who was inhaling the food in front of him as if he had had none before in his lifetime, said only, "Beer."

Chase, for his part, requested wine with a gentle "please" and was given a large flagon of red glass that was chipped on the rim. He sloshed the red wine around in his glass and emptied it, belched, red wine running down the corners of his mouth, and was rewarded with another glass, this time filled to the rim. He laughed, looked at each face seated around the table with a look of open beneficence that would quiet any displeasure and began to eat.

As he looked in Frame's direction, Frame could see that the youth's eyes looked rather bloodshot and weary. He wore the same vague smile as he chewed that he had when sitting at the café table, listlessly rolling his skateboard back and forth beside him.

Looking at him, Frame again felt quite breathless, and as if his heart were beating far too quickly to be healthy.

He stared at the boy as much as he safely could, making sure to look from time to time over at Kiki and to remark on the quality of the food, or at Elsa, to whom he mouthed the words, "thank you," to let her know how he valued her hospitality and friendship.

Once, the youth looked up just as Frame was staring at him, measuring the movements of his jaw as he worked the food. For a moment, Jameson Frame saw the boy in the coffee shop in New York, and nearly fell off his bench by trying to lean away from the reaction that potentially was to come.

But Chase only winked at the older man, and allowed his lips to turn up more broadly, into a smile that was remarkably open and friendly. As he chewed, his left hand slipped down to his stomach and slowly slipped up this sleeveless tee, exposing the perfection of his abdominal cavity and the rope of dark fur that ran down into his shorts.

He smoothed his hand over his stomach, simulating a very slow "yum yum" motion, before coyly lowering his shirt once more. Then he yawned, showing a quantity of food still in his mouth and laughed suddenly, realizing it.

"So, uh, Jimmy," he said, and all eyes flew to him. Although the boy looked directly at Frame, it took him a long moment to realize that the boy spoke to him. Jameson looked at the youth, quizzical.

"Vera says you are pretty famous, huh?"

"Well," said Jameson Frame, flustered, unsure of what to say next.

"Now, Chase, darling, don't embarrass Mr. Frame," said Elsa tenderly. She again placed a fluttering hand on Frame's own. "He is a very special man. A man of letters. Of words. A poet."

Jameson Frame thought perhaps that he heard Chase's brother snicker as he continued to eat. He was now eating the food that Chase had left on his plate when he began to speak.

The youth leaned forward, inclined himself toward Jameson Frame.

"Man," he said, one perfect eyebrow rising above the other. "A poet. Cool."

And he nodded in Frame's direction, appraising the older man.

At this juncture, Vera spoke to Elsa, "I think it's high time for salad and cheese, huh?"

The two women arose and gathered up the paper plates, which were tossed unceremoniously into the large open garbage bin by the sink in the kitchen. Elsa wandered back in with a large cracked wooden bowl in which a series of greens were mixed and Vera brought a large rough-hewn wooden tray, the top of which was wrapped in banana leaves and covered with various cheeses.

New paper plates were filled and glasses refilled.

Jameson Frame noticed that now it was the youth who stared at the older man, as if seeing some heretofore undiscovered life form. He looked over at Frame and touched his hand to his mouth.

The rest of dinner consisted of things that were either sticky, sweet or both.

Elsa, from time to time, ran into the kitchen, coming out with various things to offer. She went missing for a time, and then, after she returned, a smell of chocolate baking filled the room.

Jameson Frame drank entirely too much wine from his little tin cup, as the cup seemed to be magically refilled each time he drank from it, like something from a children's story.

From time to time Kiki or Smack or the gentleman who was dressed in something African said something in his direction. Not hearing or understanding them, Jameson Frame nodded, and, once, giggled, which seemed sufficient to satisfy the conversation.

His eyes locked once more with those of the youth at the other end of the table. The boy raised his flagon to Frame, who raised his tin cup in return. Both drank deeply. Frame sighed.

He felt the room shift as the music changed from the stereo to the sound of a soft drumbeat in the living room, where Bobo had gone while the rest continued at the table. He sat on the long, low couch, his knees up above chest level, pushing his body as best he could up and away from the deep piled cushions. Bobo's head moved from side to side and he beat out a gentle rhythm on the drum between his bare legs. His shoulders jiggled a little, giving his motions a slightly sexual rhythm. His eyes seemed sightless as they pointed into the crowd in the other room, with no sign of recognition.

Elsa went into the kitchen once more and came out with a pan of warm brownies, the scent of which had underscored the party for the last half hour. There was general cheering at the sight of the platter.

"Take one to Bobo," instructed Vera. Elsa complied, piling two onto a bunched piece of paper towel, handing the tray to Vera, who arose to serve the other guests.

Elsa walked—floated really, on the sound of the drumbeats—into the living room and fed a brownie to Bobo, a piece at a time, until the first of his brownies was gone. His head nodded in the rhythm of his drumming. She kissed him then, lightly, sweetly, first on his forehead and then on his wide and eager lips. And she began to feed him again, slowly, in small pieces, one at a time, as if to ask with each piece, "Is this enough?"

In the dining room, Vera came around the table to where Frame was sitting and said, "Alice B. Toklas brownie, Jameson?"

Happy at the mention of a familiar name, Jameson Frame helped himself, and, again finding there was no back on the bench, leaned his weight a bit onto Kiki next to him, as he began to more powerfully feel the effects of the cheap wine.

Down at the end of the table, the boys laughed and pointed at each other as they showed their chocolate teeth.

"Barf," said Chase, punching his brother on the arm.

It seemed to Jameson Frame at that moment, that some shift, at first subtle and then profound came into the room. Some heard it. Some smelled it. Some felt it, but all saw it in a profoundly moving visual effect.

For it was then, in that moment, that a golden light entered the room, filled it and filled each guest assembled with a saturating sensation of delight.

Time slowed, and the sound of the drumbeat with it.

There was the sound of darkness outside, heard from time to time, and the sound of the rumble of conversation, comprehended and, more and more, not, within the golden room. From outside the room, the ongoing, softly insistent sound of the drumbeat instructed their hearts in how and when to beat, teased breath in and out of their lungs.

Soon, they sighed as one. Jameson took his shoulder away from Kiki, who blew him a kiss as he put his head down on the table, having no other way to relieve his back.

THIRTEEN

⸎

When next Jameson Frame looked at anything, he did so apparently through a graph of branches, as if he were out on a limb high on the tree. The branches he was entangled within were long and thin, wispy but somewhat stiff.

It took quite a while until Frame became aware that the branches were, in fact, his own fingers, and that he had the power within him not only to move them—which he did, slowly, at first, much to his own amusement—but also to remove them from his face altogether. This he found to be completely hilarious.

When his head arose, it was not unlike a periscope arising from beneath the sea, and slowly scanning in a circular motion, attempting to take in all three hundred and sixty degrees around him.

He drew himself up so that his neck craned, becoming even thinner than usual. His eyes were wide, glassy circles.

"He's looking for the brownies," hissed Kiki, much to the amusement of the room.

The table had been largely cleared of people. Vera and the Frau were dancing cheek to cheek to Frank Sinatra on the reanimated stereo system. Bobo lay on the long, long couch with his head in the lap of a woman with a red cloud of hair and a top with a long, low-cut V that displayed her small breasts and hollow throat with her every movement. Bobo, it appeared, was counting her breaths, as she cooed to him and stroked his head.

Elsa gently reached out and under Frame's left arm, helping him to his feet. He was glad of this, as his time on the picnic bench had all but crippled his back. Using her arm, he pushed off from the corner of the table, got up on what somewhat surprised him to be his bare feet and tottered a step or two. Elsa walked with him and whispered, "Chase has gone out onto the front porch and he especially asked that I should tell you when you awoke."

In a velvety haze, with heavy softness coating his tongue, Frame slowly made for the door. He glanced back at Elsa as he walked two steps, three, and saw her, standing, retreating backward as he walked forward, her head bobbing sweetly, as if teaching a child to walk.

Chase took his feet off the chair with the sagging cushion so that Frame could sit. He greeted Frame casually, as if he were expected. "Hey," he said simply as the door had opened.

Frame sat down and realized that the sagging was caused by a rip in the chair's woven seat. He felt, sitting there, as if he might fall through to the porch floor at any moment. Chase either was unaware of or ignored his plight. He stared off into the darkness, his chin pointing outward from time to time.

"Mikey's out there on the canal in a rowboat," he said. "Thought I better keep an eye on him."

They sat silent for a moment. In the distance, Frame could hear quiet splashing in the water beyond.

Other sounds emerged as he listened. Music here and there, inside and out. And the sounds of televisions on multiple channels, and car radios moving toward and then past. Of electric fans and of conversations in the dark. A smattering of louder, richer sounds from the boardwalk not far away—the boardwalk that never quite slept but always, even in the darkest night, sparkled and spoke in myriad colors and voices.

Jameson Frame, perhaps buoyed by the night and the cheap wine and the Alice B. Toklas brownies, looked directly into the boy's face. Not a furtive glance, issued in pulsing regularity, as was his habit, but a direct, appraising look. Chase, seeing him, looked at him and then averted his glance, fading it into soft focus, inviting Frame to look at his leisure. He shifted a bit in his chair, perhaps to become more comfortable, perhaps to allow his face to be more fully and completely illuminated by a shaft of light that the reading lamp on the table by the window threw.

Never had Jameson Frame seen such perfection. Not in man or boy. Not in art or life. It was a face that was chiseled in desire. The skin free of mark or discoloration. The eyes, clear, deep, passionate: containing all things. Something lived within those eyes, something that, when they fell upon you, came forward from them, into you. Making a simple glance an active, even an aggressive thing.

His face had a slight lantern shape to it, with a strong jawline covered in a wire mesh of heavy beard. The beard of the sort of the perfectly tended untended type that was, at present, in style and here on display as high art. The stubble line enhancing the manly form, while the loose, disheveled hair suggested raw youth. And his eyes, again the eyes, serene and yet demanding, suggested the possibility of both.

The pointed arch of his heavy brow and the shape of his ears suggested some slight wolfishness in his make up, enhancing his masculinity. The broadness of his face and its innate symmetry enhanced his beauty, as did his perfect, strong, almost-too-big nose. A nose with a hint of the aquiline about it.

If the source of his shifting personal power lay in his eyes, the source of the Nile that was his beauty was in his lips. Lips that countered everything else on his face. Full, feminine lips that pouted and purred, that were colored a perfectly, ridiculously pinkish pink and shaped in a flapper's cupid's bow. Placed within the context of his dark masculinity—the purest white skin set against jet black hair that disappeared, along with the inky mesh of his scruff, in the night—the pinky pink lips, a set that might have been dubbed kissable in a television commercial were they located in a teen-aged blonde's face, were utterly, shockingly, endlessly enchanting when placed within the hard-jawed face of the youth.

In repose, the perfection of his head, the shape of it, the regularity of the features, the coloring—Snow White with a penis—was only enhanced by this completely ridiculous mouth, one that issued the equally ridiculous voice.

And yet, it, all of it, only enhanced the unique beauty of *him*.

There was, of course, more than a hint of the body under the clothes. His body issued heat.

The boy, Frame noticed, had shifted forward during his reverie. He sat now hunched forward in his direction, looking him in the eye, his own eyes filled with a most decorous mirth.

From the outer darkness, Mikey splashed. Chase ignored him. He brought his face closer.

"You want to see my tattoos?" he asked.

Without waiting for an answer, Chase slowly pulled his shirt off over his head and turned his back. He brought a hand around as best he could, his face smashed against his shoulder, and pointed to an intricate cross etched onto the upper part of his back. As his face moved downward, his hair fell perfectly, grazing his eyes.

"This was my first tattoo," he said, "I got it when I was like fourteen." He moved as he spoke, bringing his body around to face front again. "It's an Irish cross. I got it because I am Irish and Scottish and Welsh and Swedish or something. Pure whitey white."

"Then I got this one." He brought his leg up and placed it in Frame's nervous lap, showing him up close the same tattoo that he had seen before. The Maori tattoo.

"It's aboriginal."

"Maori, actually."

"Huh?"

"It's not of Australian design, but rather from New Zealand. From the Maori people."

"Yeah? Cool." He flexed his foot in Frame's lap, showing the dirt on his sole, and brought his knee around a bit to look again at his own tattoo, as if he had not seen it before, digging his toes into Frame's thigh as he did so.

His face moved forward and he looked up at Jameson Frame, a smile crawling from ear to ear.

"Thanks, man. Good to know."

And Chase revealed the rest of his tattoos for Frame, moving in a succession of poses in something of a dance, as clothing shifted and tales of the reason for and the amount of pain caused by each tattoo was conspiratorially shared.

He ended by showing Frame the instep of his left foot. There a tattoo filled the whole of the foot and written was one word: *Invincible*.

"I got it when I was skateboarding. I was just tearing along, not paying enough attention to what I was doing. I was maybe sixteen at the time.

And I fell and I fractured my foot. It hurt like fucking hell and took a long time to heal. But when it got better I had the tattoo done. It reminds me that I am not as big a deal as I think." He nodded, shook his head and, laughing lightly at himself, brought his face up close to Frame's.

"Where's Mikey?" Chase whispered, shaping each word with his cupid bow mouth.

Mikey was found easily enough, as he had fallen asleep inside the little red rowboat. The boat, still tied to the dock, lightly bounced up against the dock and off again, each time with a dull thud. Each time, Mikey matched the sound with a snore of his own. He lay with his legs spread out in front of him, one tipped into the canal water, one hand on his stomach and the other splayed behind him. His mouth hung open as he slept. In the night, the pale tone of his skin gave him a ghostly pallor against the red of the boat.

To awaken his brother, Chase put his invincible foot down onto the boat, and rocked it. Gently at first and then harder, calling softly, "Mikey? Mikey Mike Mike Mike Mikey?" Until the younger boy awakened. "It's time to get up," he said to his brother. He then helped him gently out of the boat and spoke to Frame over his shoulder. "I have to take Mikey somewhere," he said. "You want to come along?" And he, rather eagerly, Frame thought, motioned with his head toward the row of parked cars.

"Elsa," said Frame. "Vera. I'm their guest."

"Oh, they won't mind. Just tell them I offered to drive you back to your hotel."

Chase and Mikey walked over to an ancient blue Ford Falcon that was wedged partially onto the lawn.

"Go." He motioned to the house. "We'll wait for you here."

Still sleepy, Mikey opened the rear door of the car and hurled himself face down inside. Chase closed the door after him, after checking to see if his feet were in.

Jameson Frame walked back into the house to see Bobo and Kiki slowly, deeply kissing on the near end of the couch. Neither looked up as he entered.

He managed to find his shoes and to slip his feet into them, but his coat was nowhere in sight. He walked into the kitchen where Elsa was dragging an oversized plastic trash bag toward the back door. Looking at Jameson Frame, she asked, "Are you going? But it's so early . . ."

"Ah, the young man, Chase, offered me a ride to my hotel."

"Oh, Chase is such a good boy. You must be sure to ask him about his work, you know. He is very special."

"I will." He bent to kiss her and to thank her for the evening. She accepted his kiss on her cheek with a sweet smile. She smelled of chocolate and lavender and other fragrant things. "Ah, one thing," he said, rising to full height. "My coat."

"Oh, did you have a coat?" She asked, her index finger to her lips. "Oh, but of course you did, your beautiful suit. We must institute a search party."

Thinking of Kiki and Bobo and the other guests in varying degrees of post-party intimacy, and of Chase, who was outside waiting, Frame hesitated.

"I can get it later," he said in a somewhat higher pitch than usual. "It's not important."

"Are you sure, Jameson? It is a small house . . ."

"Will you bring it with you when next we meet?"

"Most certainly, Jameson."

He was backing rather hurriedly toward the door. "Thank Vera for me."

"Most assuredly, Jameson."

"And thanks again," he said, opening the door.

"Good night, Jameson," she said with a tone of resigned finality.

Outside, Mikey's feet were sticking out the window on the driver's side of the back seat. They moved in rhythm with a song that was playing on the car radio.

"Mother let you go, did she?" Chase asked as Frame tipped his head in through the car window. "Get in."

No sooner had Jameson Frame closed his door than the car burst off into the night, fast and, with a simple touch of the radio control, loud.

FOURTEEN

~

Night, Jameson Frame noticed, his head leaning against the hard metal of the car's window frame, hair rushing at his face, flew by much more quickly while driving in Los Angeles than it did in his native New York. Here, there was no long column of nighttime traffic, lights, colored and clear, blinding you in all directions.

Here the cars on the city streets were few. The only lines of traffic to be seen were on the highways that they passed. Seldom did they stop for a traffic light.

When they did, Chase inevitably used the opportunity to change the music.

At one light, he asked Frame if he had ever heard of a band named "Banshee."

When Frame admitted that he had not, in fact, ever heard them or heard of them, the boy prepared to slip the disc into the stereo.

His foot on the gas as the light changed, Chase glanced over at the man.

"Hey, you're not over sixty, are you?"

"No, I'm not. Why?"

"Because I think that if you were, this just might kill you."

And he turned up the speakers as high as they would go. The sounds of death and eternal torment, or some approximation thereof, filled the car.

Chase flipped his head forward and back in joyful collaboration with the music. He beat his right hand against the steering wheel.

Mikey stirred in the back seat and sat back up, looking like a child just arising for the morning alarm. He rubbed his eyes and grinned. "Hey," he said, "Banshee!"

They had, throughout the time they had been driving, Frame noticed, sticking his head out the side window in order to absorb some of the sound of Banshee playing, been travelling from the ocean into the city's urban core. The buildings now were higher, making the streets ahead and behind them darker, more foreboding. Chase seemed aware of where he was and where he was heading. He took turns somewhat ambitiously and pushed his bare foot furiously onto the gas pedal, jerking the car ahead in whiplash motion.

Feelings of unease began to penetrate the haze surrounding Jameson Frame. His eyes narrowed as he studied the buildings rushing by. The ocean-front palaces had given way to office buildings, which had, only recently, yielded the landscape to warehouses and abandoned storefronts. At a dark corner with a streetlamp out, Chase took a roaring right-hand turn. Instantly, he turned the headlights up high and slowed the car to a stop as it neared a dead end.

"Okay, Mikey, we're here," he said, switching off the car stereo. Silence.

Mikey looked around, recognized the place and nodded. He got out of the car, waved and disappeared into the darkness.

"You cool, Bro?" asked Chase.

He was answered by the sound of a door slamming shut.

"He's cool," said Chase to Frame. He paused a moment, as if unsure to whom it was that he spoke. Then his perfect grin appeared once more and he pressed his face into Frame's personal space.

"Where to now?" he asked, backing the car at full speed out of the alley onto the street. He pointed the car in the direction from which they had come and barreled off, cackling. "I have just one more stop before I take you back to the hotel, okay?"

"Fine," said Jameson Frame, who leaned his head again on the frame of the window so that he could simultaneously watch the oncoming road and Chase's face as they drove.

With the music off, Frame soon felt himself being lulled into sleep by the motion of the car and the feel of the wind, rich with ocean scent, blowing against his face. As he drifted away, the last image that he had was of Chase's face, and his eyes in the rear-view mirror.

Those eyes were again the first thing he saw upon awakening.

"Jimmy," the boy whispered, his face up close once again. "We're here."

From within his fogged state, Frame heard the boy calling, as if from a great distance. In his dream, he ran toward the voice, down corridors, through a maze of hallways, all dimly lit, but he could not reach its source. When his dream burst around intrusive reality and he saw the boy's eyes looking into his, the older man without realizing it lifted his right hand and touched the boy's cheek.

Chase let it linger there a second, and then gently removed the hand with his own.

"I said we're here," he repeated.

Frame stretched and blinked and made himself as alert as possible. He looked at his exquisite wristwatch and saw that it was now after 1:00 a.m. He heard the driver's door open and slam and looked out his window.

He saw a row of shops and restaurants and bars, all still open. Not Venice, but not unlike it. As with Venice the sound and the smell of the ocean was nearby. Santa Monica, perhaps?

"Are we in Santa Monica?" he asked, getting out of the car. He began to try and roll the window up to lock it.

"Leave it, man. Just leave it," said Chase, slapping his hand away and shoving the door closed. He turned and walked toward the shops.

Frame thought, when he had turned his back to him, he heard the boy continue, saying, "Just like my mother."

They stood in front of a storefront that had a bright neon sign, each letter in it a different dynamic color, each lit individually, so the word seemed to flow across the storefront. The rippling word was Tattoo.

"This won't take long, Jimmy. I wanted to get here when Bucky was here. I only like to get my ink from Bucky."

He seemed to sense Frame's hesitation from the way the older man lingered at the door.

"Come on," he said. "It's great. The guy's a fuckin' artist!"

And he went into the dingy shop and walked across the room. As he went, he took his shirt off over his head and stuffed the top of it into the top of his shorts. He then threw himself down in an elderly armchair with a chintz cover and put his feet up on the table in front of him. He picked up the large book of tattoos from the coffee table and began to study the pages.

When Frame still lingered by the door, Chase looked directly at him and beckoned him with his hand. "You're embarrassing me, Jimmy," he said with a tone of voice that Frame had heard the younger man use with his brother Mikey.

Frame, pulling his shirttails out of his pants and unbuttoning a couple of top buttons, walked across the room and took the seat next to Chase. From the light of an overhead can, he could see the rise and fall of the youth's perfectly muscled abdomen, while still pretending to study the pages displaying various tattoos.

"Be with you in a few," said a squat, heavily muscled man with a scarf tied tightly around the top of his head and numerous chains attached to various piercings here and there on his body.

"Okay, Bro," called back Chase in his high boyish voice.

He turned to Frame, his finger mashed down into the book. "This one, Jimmy," he said. "I'm going to get the anchor."

Then he closed the book and shoved it into Frame's hands.

"What about you?"

Without giving Frame a chance to object, the boy continued, "Come on, we'll do it together. It's great, you'll see." He spread the book open across Frame's lap, moving in close to look at the pictures with him.

"I've heard it is very painful," Frame said slowly in a measured tone.

"Nah, not that much, not really," said Chase, while fumbling through the pocket of his shorts. "Besides, this really helps. You won't feel a thing."

He had produced a fat hand-rolled cigarette from his pocket, along with a pack of matches. He lit the joint and inhaled deeply, and motioned for Frame to draw near. He did and Chase brought his mouth over close—close to the point of nearly touching—to his own and exhaled the pungent smoke slowly into the man's mouth. He closed his cupid's lips and drew back, smiling.

Frame drew the thick smoke into his lungs and clung on to it. Held onto it as long as he could, and exhaled finally. Chase, who had had a puff or two in the meantime, handed Frame the joint. Frame touched his lips to the wet edge of the butt, inhaled and again let the thick smoke swirl within his chest. He felt warm from it, and from the nearness of the boy.

"Hey," said Chase, his foot grinding into Frame's leg. "You could get 'Invincible' like me."

"Could," said Frame, coughing lightly. "Not." He coughed some more. "The best I could do is 'Vincible,' I'm afraid." His coughing mixed with laughter.

The boy laughed along, slapped Jameson Frame lightly on his arm. "Then do that, Jimmy. Do that do that do that . . ."

The sight of the boy's gleaming face filled all the world for Jameson Frame.

"All right, then," he said with a bit of a sigh.

"All right, then, Jimmy."

Very soon they were seated in straight-backed chairs back behind the bead curtain in the back of the store. While Bucky, the muscular squat man with a sweaty bandanna tied across his forehead, prepared Chase's arm for the tattoo work, having determined that the boy wanted a sailor's anchor placed on the inside of his left arm, just below the elbow, a young woman with a piercing in her nose who was introduced to him as Alice prepared Frame for his first ink. They had had him sign some form, and, somehow, without discussing it, it was determined that he would put the cost of both tattoos on his credit card, which had already been run through the machine, and now he sat with his left pant leg rolled, waiting for the pain to begin.

When it came, it was like lightning carving a path underneath his skin. Tears in his eyes, he reached out a hand to Chase, who, standing there with his left arm bent in a protective stance, only laughed and said, "Hurts like hell, don't it, Jimmy?"

Alice took the offered hand and cooed at Frame, saying, "Relax, mister, just relax," in a sing-song voice.

"No, no, no, no, no," Frame burbled, spit coming to the corners of his mouth, tears running down his face.

"No?" asked Bucky looking up.

Frame looked for, but could not see Chase.

The needle lifted from his hot skin.

"What you want me to do?" asked Bucky.

Frame looked down at his leg, expecting to see a massive wound. Instead, he saw what looked like a short line, as if a child with a pen had drawn on his skin. Groggy, he felt what was perhaps a misplaced sense of chagrin.

"What can we make of it?" Frame asked. "Make of it easily?"

"I got a pretty good start on the 'V.'"

"Make a 'V' then. A nice big capital 'V' and we'll chalk it up to Venice." And he reached for and took Alice's hand while the needle penetrated his dry skin. And she held him tight and held him still through the brief time it took Bucky to shape the single letter.

When it was finished, a beautifully shaped Roman V faced downward along the inside portion of his left calf muscle. Somewhat inflamed and certainly swollen, it stood in bas-relief against the rest of his skin. His eyes clearing, Jameson looked for Chase, who was nowhere to be seen. Pushing up from his chair in a sudden panic, he dodged Alice and began toward the door. He loudly refused both the bandage and the Bactine that Bucky offered him, in his belief that, like Mikey, he had been abandoned. The pain forced him to keep his pant leg rolled and caused him to walk with a limp.

He moved as quickly as he could, outside into the night, where he found Chase, as he hoped he would—his heart beating wildly against the possibility that he was alone in the night—leaning against the side of his car and smoking a cigarette. Without a word, the young man got into the car and started the engine. Cowed, Frame got into the passenger seat beside him.

They drove to Venice in silence. From time to time, Chase blew on his bandaged arm or stuck it outside the window seeking relief from his own discomfort.

Finally, Chase spoke.

"What did you end up getting?"

"A rather nice 'V' to always remind me of Venice."

"That was a good idea. Stick with the little ones, Jimmy," he said. "That one almost killed me." And he indicated an intricate multi-patterned tattoo that started on the upper part of the inside of his left arm and crossed down his flank and back. "That was done in three layers and I never could get it to look right," he said. "Mikey had to hold my head still while they were doing the last part to keep me from moving." He tried to shift around to show Frame exactly what he meant but soon gave up.

When they arrived at the hotel, it was nearly three. They parked the car around the corner and walked together into the lobby. In his mind's eye, Jameson Frame suddenly saw himself as others must see him—the man who had left the building only a few hours ago in a smart silk suit and a clean, crisp shirt, was now returning limping, with his pant leg rolled, his leg swollen by a tattoo, his shirttail out and shirt unbuttoned, and his own eyes, no doubt, red and bleary from the drugs. Which reminded him of how he surely must smell.

In spite of it all, the desk staff managed to welcome their guest home with aplomb and merely glanced in Chase's direction discreetly.

"Oh, he's with me," said Frame in something like his usual arid fashion.

As the doors of the elevator closed on them, the two collapsed together in laughter. They walked down the hall together toward Frame's room, Frame wondering with each succeeding footfall how much closer they would get before the boy excused himself back into the elevator.

He put his keycard into the door and opened it, moving aside to allow Chase to enter.

The boy walked in, assessed the space of the sitting room and wandered into the bedroom. When Frame caught up with him, he was sitting on the bed, his long legs stretched out and wide open.

"Pretty cool, Jimmy," he said. "I could learn to like a place like this."

Noticing the various boxes of electrical goods scattered about, he asked, "What's this?" His full attention shifted from the bed to the new computer equipment. He went out into the front room again, to the desk by the window, to look at the new laptop. "Hey, Jimmy," he said, with something like awe in his voice, "this is the best they make."

"So I was told," said Frame.

The boy turned the computer on. The screen flickered and then filled with the factory-suggested wallpaper.

"Have you seen my website yet?" asked Chase.

"Why, no. I didn't know you had one."

"Go sit down, I'll bring it to you."

Frame sat on the couch watching, as the boy, hunched over the desktop, typed more quickly than Frame would have imagined. He stood and waited for the screen to load. "Come on, come on," he said under his breath. And, with the site fully loaded, he brought the laptop over to Frame and sat on the couch next to him.

Frame frowned at the little letters in the address line of the site. Chaseme.com. Finally, he said, "Chase me?"

"Dot com," said the boy. "Chase me dot com. That's my domain. And this is my mission statement." He pointed to the screen.

Frame read, "I Want to Share My Whole Life With You. Let's Make Art."

"What does it mean, Chase?" the man asked.

"You just have to read it, Jimmy. It's, like, something completely new and cutting edge. But I make my art here like you do with your poems." Frame could not, in spite of himself, help but notice the boy pronounced the word as "poms."

He glanced down the page and saw, to his amazement, myriad pictures of Chase in states of undress, many in underwear. He lifted the computer for a closer look.

"Oh, yeah," said Chase, "I used to do that, too, model underwear. I still do sometimes, but I don't have a job right now. Right now this site is what I am doing. Making art."

As the boy spoke, Frame felt his eyes moist with oncoming tears at the idea of such art and the foolishness of those who would identify it as such. He felt, in that moment, a sense of tenderness all too rare for him, mixed with a sensation of lust that bore its way up from deep in his bowels. And then he thought, quite suddenly, of Elsa and her practical bangs and her gentle touch and wanted to tell her, all in that moment, how very much he appreciated her for her gift to him of this, this very moment, this place and this possibility.

Even as he felt the wash of emotion sweep over him, he heard the boy again, asking him for his promise that he would look at the site, *promise me that you will, you will won't you, Jimmy . . .*

"I will," he said, hearing in his own voice a timber of sweetness he had not heard before.

Chase stood, and, with this sign, Frame followed and they walked together toward the door. Frame opened it. The boy walked through and then turned again so that the two were very close. Their faces paused, Frame's eyes closed. He felt the boy's breath on his face. Felt his face come closer still.

The boy lightly touched the tip of his perfect nose against Frame's and traced across it and down, so that the tip of it touched Frame's lips. The older man kissed it softly and the boy then poked his nose once, twice into the center of Frame's closed, pillowed mouth. And the youth lifted his chin and kissed Jameson Frame very sweetly on his forehead, placing his hands on either side of Frame's face as he did so.

The boy backed away. "Goodnight, Jimmy," he said simply. And he walked toward the elevator.

FIFTEEN

❧

Jameson Frame closed the door with arms that felt at once weak and curiously heavy. His leg ached and itched. His body was covered in perspiration.

He unbuckled his belt and pulled it from his pants, which he then unfastened and let fall to the floor. Stepping out of them, he lifted his left leg so that his foot was wedged against the top of the coffee table and looked down to see the beautiful, placid V surrounded by an angry red mound of flesh. He poked at it, gently. It throbbed. It itched. How he wanted to scratch it, to rip at the reddened skin. Instead, he blew on it softly and felt how that, too, increased the ongoing pulsation beneath the angry letter.

Frame sat on the couch, arranging himself carefully so that his leg touched nothing, spreading that left leg wide into the center of the room. He looked down at his shiny new computer, whose screen, though dimmed, still showed the front page of Chase's site: *I Want To Share My Whole Life With You.*

He touched the track pad and the screen glowed bright. From the light of the screen in the nearly darkened room—the desk lamp the only other thing illuminated in the whole of the suite—he suddenly realized that, among the numerous pictures of Chase modeling various fits and forms of underwear (each picture accompanied by a paragraph or two extolling not only the product, but also the photographer whose work the picture was), there were a large number of nudes as well.

Frame leaned forward. His right hand came up to his mouth and twisted his lips as he pulled at his face. His brow frowned in concentration. With his left hand, he traced the outline of one of the photos with the cursor. As it touched the picture on the screen, the tiny dark arrow was transformed into white hand with a pointing finger. Frame clicked where the finger pointed and, in an instant, the photo filled the entire page.

In the glow of the screen, Frame's eyes were illuminated in a moment of joy that soon yielded to a period of lust. In front of him, on the screen, was a picture in which Chase—the very Chase who, only minutes ago, had kissed him on the forehead and who, only minutes before that had sat on his bed in the darkened room and beckoned him come—rested himself on a couch with pillows propped all around him. His arms were behind his head, his neck was thrust forward as his head fell back, his hair askew, his Adam's apple dominant. He wore an old flannel shirt, two or three sizes too small, that pulled at his frame, his shoulders. The shirt was open in front, exposing the young man's perfectly carved chest. The wild foliage of dark hair, here and there. The soft mounds of his nipples. The perfect washboard of an abdomen.

Beneath the tails of the shirt, Chase was perfectly naked. Nude—as this was, by the look of it, and by Chase's own definition of it, art and not pornography. Therefore, the phallus, which hung in rather a torpid state between the young man's legs, showed no rigor, only masculinity, as did the large, pendulous sack behind it.

The legs, the perfect legs traveled off the screen into the void.

The boy's face was, in this picture, vacant in repose, something that Jameson Frame had never seen. The face presented the body here as an offering, as something to be seen and witnessed and shared.

Frame stared at the screen for a long time, feeling his own body's response to the iconography on the screen.

He clicked again and the picture shrank. He looked down the page, clicking here and there, seeing a timeline of Chase from a youthful and, relatively speaking, chubby boy a few years before, who stood like the men in the Sears catalog who, like him, were modeling underthings, to the man Chase, whose eyes lived in three dimensions on the two-dimensional screen.

A box promised a video and Frame clicked on it.

And over a bed of music, Chase danced for him. A nude figure of Chase undulated in front of a camera in a video that was edited in quick cuts and shadows. So that the entirety of his figure was never seen, but the effect was tremendously erotic.

The video lasted merely two minutes. Frame played it again and again. In the end, only the vast sense of exhaustion that overtook him could have stopped him from watching.

Not quite sure of how to turn the computer off, Frame closed the lid, saw the white light still winking at him like an eye and turned it so that the light faced the rear cushions of the couch.

He then pointed himself at the bed and hurled himself toward it. He hit it full on, his torso falling against the mattress in a belly smack, his newly tattooed leg touching down. With a wince and a yelp, he threw the leg off the bed and quickly passed out.

Frame awakened, seemingly only moments later. His mouth felt dry, his tongue lacquered against the roof of his mouth.

He awoke, he found, to the sound of drumming. A sound that at first he had assumed was inside his own head. But, as he became more alert, he realized it was coming from the beach outside. He further realized that the sun was indeed shining and that more than moments had passed.

He rolled over on his back, groaning with the effort, and stared up at the ceiling, listening to the sound of drums and whistles down below. When again his left leg touched the bed, Frame winced and jumped a little. He then remembered, as if from a book he'd read or a film seen, the tattoo. Frame was dismayed to find that he indeed was the possessor of the Roman V and that it was the source of a pulsation that followed more or less the pounding of the drum.

Sitting up, he found that he was incredibly hungry and that this hunger would need to be very soon appeased. He called down to room service and, instead of wanting oatmeal and juice, he ordered eggs, steak, potatoes, toast, coffee and a large Bloody Mary. And told the staff to hurry.

He wandered into the bath and washed. He looked into the mirror and was somewhat aghast to find an unshaven middle-aged man with circles under his eyes and a somewhat pinched expression looking back at him. He looked close at the red veins that mapped his eyes and went into the bedroom again in search of his sunglasses. Finding them, he put them on and sat on the bed in his day-old underwear and shirt to await room service.

Jameson Frame ripped at the bloody steak with the knife he was provided. He smashed the yellow of his fried eggs with the toast points, allowing the yellow and red to mix together before he dragged the toast through it once more and punched it into his mouth. He laughed.

Down below he could see the source of the drumbeats, as Bobo and assorted other musicians had formed a large circle on the sand, within which various locals, artists and vacationers took turns dancing and shouting under the ever-present sun.

Frame drank his coffee black, as he seemed to lack the ability for the fine motions required to pour cream and measure sugar. It tasted bitter and strong. He drank the scalding liquid in large gulps, slurping it in. Again he laughed.

After taking the best shower he could take, given the new tattoo, Frame walked out, studied himself briefly in the mirror in the hallway, shook his head, and wondered what he might wear today.

Given the fact that his leg would in no way tolerate the feel of cloth against it, Frame took up the shears in his shaving kit and transformed his silk trousers into shorts and donned clean boxers (which showed a bit under the poorly cut shorts) and a clean white undershirt. He again slipped his bare feet into his shoes and made for the door, leaving the electronics boxes strewn about, the computer on the couch, the bed a mass of sweaty sheets and the breakfast tray out on the balcony.

He walked in a straight line from the lobby to the circle out on the sand. Along the way, he heard his name called from many throats. "Good morning, Mr. Frame," from the man behind the registration desk, "Jameson Frame, good morning to you!" from the doorman, "Jameson" here and "Frame" there from folks in the café, on the boardwalk, and finally, and most rigorously, from Bobo, who sat behind a mighty conga drum, providing quick access to jerking hip actions for the myriad folks who had joined the circle. Some played bits of stick and bone and metal that they had found in the sand. Others merely waved their hands at the morning sun and briefly shaded each other's eyes.

"Good morning, Jameson Frame," sang Bobo to the island rhythms that his hands shaped on the skin of the drum. "We greet thee with this circle. It is for you and for this glorious sun."

And the circle opened for him, and, tightening, looped round him several times, closing in upon him like a boa about to feast. And he raised his arms up over his head and spun against the current, feeling the flow of flesh against his as the multitude gyrated, carving a spontaneous Catherine wheel in the dirty sand.

As the drum circle broke up and Bobo loaded his instruments onto a rickshaw and pulled them on down the boardwalk to his regular workspace a few hundred yards away, Jameson Frame made his way to the outdoor café.

There, Vera and Elsa were having hot chocolate and splitting a brioche.

"It looks to me that our friend Jameson Frame has gone native," said Vera to Elsa as Frame came into earshot.

He looked down at his wardrobe and grinned at the two of them, standing with his arms slightly out away from his body like a paper doll.

He sat then, emptied the sand from his shoes, and thanked them again for the evening before.

"Wonderful evening, Jameson," said Elsa. "Largely because of your attendance."

"Now I understand that young Chase was obliging enough to give you a ride home?" said Vera, looking at him over the top of her enormous black-framed sunglasses that she pulled down to the tip of her nose with her index finger.

Elsa inclined her face a bit to hear his answer.

"Why, yes. He did."

"And did you boys go straight back home?"

"Why," said Jameson Frame, "no. Not exactly."

And he lifted his leg where he sat and showed them.

"A tattoo?" asked Elsa.

"A tattoo of . . . a 'V,'" said Vera.

Frame flushed and slipped his leg down, until it crossed the other at the knee.

"It is a very pretty 'V,'" said Elsa. "Such a pretty thing and how clever."

The waiter came over. Frame ordered hot chocolate and a brioche with butter.

There was silence at the table, except for the sounds of the ocean and the crowd, until his meal arrived.

As he took a sip of the hot sweet liquid, Elsa asked, "Jameson, do you remember the matter that we were discussing only yesterday. The matter of the crow's-feet?"

"The what?" asked Frame.

"Those slight imperfections, here," and she used the tip of her little finger to locate where they might be on the left side of the eyes of her own face, "and here," she added, touching lightly the outside corner of her right eye.

"Oh, for heaven's sake, the laugh lines. That's what they're called. The lines by your eyes, Jameson," Vera said sharply.

"What about them?" Frame asked as he broke the roll in two and buttered it.

"I thought that while you were here, you might want to correct those imperfections and so I took the step of calling Dr. Magellan." Else whispered as if she feared violence.

"He's her man. He's the best. If you count his clients, he has more Academy Awards than DreamWorks," said Vera. "And she's just trying to be helpful, so be nice."

"I'm sorry, Elsa," he said. "I don't mean to be snappish. It's just that I had such a little sleep."

Elsa and Vera exchanged a meaningful glance.

"And don't think that it doesn't show," said Vera. "Look at the circles under your eyes . . ."

Jameson Frame set down the bite of roll that was headed toward his mouth. He looked at her.

She took off her sunglasses.

"Well, it's simple math, Jameson," she said, looking him dead in the eye. After you get to be a certain age, well, you can't go running around until dawn with the young lovelies and get up the next morning looking like they do." She put her sunglasses back on again and looked out at the ocean. "At least not without some help."

There was a pause. Jameson ate a bite of the roll. "So, this Dr. Magellan. He would be the man to see about this sort of thing."

"He is the best, Jameson. He is an artist." There was another pause.

"And he is willing to see you at one o'clock," Elsa concluded.

Frame, somewhat startled, nodded his head, assessing.

"She pulled strings for you, Jameson," said Vera in a warning tone.

"How long does that give us?" he asked, looking down at his exquisite watch.

"Oh, finish your cocoa," said Vera. "We have plenty of time."

He leaned back a bit and put his arm up on a rail. He noticed that his leg continued to throb.

"We have enough time to stop at a lovely men's shop that is on the way, if you like, Jameson," said Elsa, noticing the cut of his shorts.

Frame began to protest, but remembering the demise of his silk suit, he decided in that moment, that perhaps it was time to find something new, something perhaps more youthful.

"Well, all right!" he said jovially. He raised his cocoa cup to them and they toasted.

"To new clothes and no wrinkles," he said.

"To youth," Vera corrected.

And they finished their drinks.

And Jameson Frame arose.

"I should go and get ready. Shall we meet here at ten? Will that be enough time?"

"I should think so," said Elsa.

"I will call a taxi to meet us."

"A taxi, Jameson? All the way to Beverly Hills in a taxi?" Vera interjected, her voice deep with horror. "I should think we would be far more comfortable in a town car." She stared at him, as Elsa looked at him with a vague, sweet expression on her face.

Jameson Frame bowed to them.

"Then we shall go by town car."

SIXTEEN

‍

Jameson Frame sat at his perfectly appointed desk. He looked up and out the window to the Pacific beyond. He looked down at the pristine keyboard of his new computer. On the screen was an electronic replica of a blank page. A small, thin line marked his progress on the page, blinking slowly.

He sat dressed in the thick, wide cotton shorts usually worn by those journeying up the Amazon or on the search for the source of the Nile. He had a short-sleeved shirt of the softest linen and new sandals made of honey-colored leather. Around the top of the calf muscle of his left leg, he wore a gauze bandage that was held in place with surgical tape.

On the desk in front of and to the right of his shiny laptop was a gin martini in a clean, new, crystal glass.

He looked at his exquisite watch in order to plan his time, looked again at the sea, sighed, and turned his attention to the screen in front of him.

On the top of the page was that title that he had selected some time before, "The Waters of Venice, California." On the page was nothing else.

Enjoying again the spring of the keys, he wrote:

Were I in the business of transforming the reality of memoir into the art of fiction, I might, in this particular case, be drawn into the use of prose at its most purple and say that, in my short time here, my experience in toto has been one of seduction. That the very air that is breathed here intoxicates, not from salt, but from seduction of a most wanton sort.

And, indeed, I must admit it. I have, in my way, been seduced.

Also this place is notable for its filth. In the Venice of Italy, another place in which grime, even plague, underlies the face of promiscuity, the filth originates in the dank, sordid waters of the canals.

Here, where the canals are bright, happy suggestions of the original, the foulness arises another way. Here, the sands upon which the town itself was built are themselves the carriers of, and most certainly the ultimate source of, every kind of muck.

One puts one's hand out into the sand and comes away with hepatitis from a needle buried in a shallow, sandy grave. One chooses to sun himself upon the sand and feels, when reclining, a sort of oiliness, a putrid viscous layer peeling off the surface of the sand and onto one's skin.

Whatever the source—sand, sun or water, the endless, fathomless, unthinkable churning mass that is the water, which, so much more blatantly than the subversive dark waters of the original Venice threatens us with upheaval, threatens to consume us all—the simple truth is that, as with seduction, I have sampled the filth.

I descended into it last night. Descended into it and then I reveled in it. Slept in it when I might have chosen to wash. This morning, I worshiped it, my heathen arms thrown upward to the sun.

I have been dazzled by all that is around me; I have begun to yearn. I have allowed myself to reach for what I wanted and to be kissed by it with an oddly Puritan kiss. Have riddled my way through the nature of desire. And can but posit, as a result, the meaning of desire when that desired defines perfection and embodies it.

> But How Can I Praise the Perfect Curve
> Of Cupid's Bow
> And In My Praising Feel Bliss
> If Truth To Tell
> From Cupid's Bow
> My Most Perfect Desire
> Is a Kiss?

Frame rested his chin on the palm of his right hand. Then reached for and took a sip of his drink.

Kiss, Ha! He thought to himself. *If only it were as easy as this weak-kneed greeting card verse implied.*

He felt, as he so often did when his fingers rested on the keyboard of his red Selectric, that there was some sort of barrier between himself and his words. That, if he could but push through that barrier, he might be able to better, more honestly write something fine.

He took a slug of his drink. It burned against his throat. He began again. He wrote:

I found myself amazed, not many hours ago, upon returning here to my suite, having set the time to meet my two lady friends again for a trip into town. I opened the door hesitantly, not wanting to see what I had made of my suite in these last two days, but, instead, found the place transformed.

I found my front room in a state of perfect calm and order. My computer had been taken from where I threw it last night and placed on the desk and plugged in, so that it charged itself while awaiting my use.

I found the bed changed and made new. A perfect plane with a soft down comforter at the bottom, rolled and set to perfection. My clothing had been discreetly gathered into a laundry bag in the closet, with tags for wash and for dry clean set neatly in place, and, clipped to them, a pen.

And the many boxes in which my new electronic purchases had been made were not to be found. In their place was a sweet note telling me that they were being kept safe for me, stored, prepared for my departure whenever that time might come and that, should I want them, I need only dial housekeeping from any of the phones in my suite.

Indeed, even the temperature of the rooms had been made perfect. The same hands that straightened all else also closed the door to the balcony, allowing the room to return to the same pristine state in which I had originally found it.

It was then that I went into my bath, saw my beautiful thick white robe hanging on the back of the door, closed it, and turned the water in the shower on, hard and hot. I dropped my clothing to the floor and prepared to climb into the shower bath.

Realizing at the last moment that, once clean, once sterilized of the filth that covered both my clothing and myself, I would never again want to touch the clothing in that pile, I ran naked to it, scooped it up to my chest, and ran with it back to the laundry bag in the closet.

I fished my wallet out of the shorts I cut from the pants of my silk suit, realizing suddenly that Elsa had failed to bring me the jacket this morning. I stuffed all of it into the bag, tying it as tight as I could. I then lifted the laundry bag, the tags and the pen and threw all into the trashcan in the hallway off my bedroom by the closet door and went back into the bathroom and locked the door behind me, as if, during the hot shower, the filthy rags would rise up and attack.

I cannot say how long I stayed in there, as I had long since lost track of time. I do remember that I scrubbed my skin perhaps as I never have before. Scrubbed layer after layer. I took care only not to further enrage the V, the brand that I had given myself the night before, which still causes me no small amount of pain. But wash I did, even there, and everywhere else on my body, scrubbing hard with the washcloth and then again with the fine bathing sponge the hotel provided, with skin soap and then with shampoo, until again I began to feel as if I might know myself should I again pass a mirror and catch sight of my own haggard face.

I stood under the wonderful wide scalding hot flow and then, spontaneously, made the water quite cold, making noises not unlike the seals in the Pacific as the icy rain washed down on me. I felt alive in that moment, my body the very definition of clean, in a way quite similar to the way I had the night before, when the inked needle first penetrated my flesh. In both moments, shock presented herself at first to be a thrill. But in both moments, thrill was pushed aside by discomfort.

And so, I turned the temperature gauge again to bring the waters back to a calming warmth, nothing more, and, feeling quite blissful, I leaned against the wonderful tile of the shower room, feeling a sense of peace in my heart.

I had no sooner turned the water off at last and donned my wonderful white robe than I heard the phone ring and answered it. I was told that my car and my friends had both arrived and that my friends were waiting for me in the car as I had sent it on to pick them up first. I said I was on my way, hung up the phone and hurried.

With no time to think, I stepped into a lovely pair of blue trousers, a white tennis shirt, simple belt and leather tennis shoes that I had recently purchased for the trip. With the pants on, I could feel my left leg again smarting, but, reaching for my wallet, wristwatch and sunglasses, I decided that I was more than prepared to overlook it at this time.

What can I tell you about Elsa and her friend Vera? It seems to me that there is surely so much to know. And yet, I must admit that anything I might state here would be conjecture as the two have managed, while even inviting me into their home, to actually reveal to me no details whatsoever of their existence.

For instance, how do the two manage at all times and on all days to be free and unencumbered by work or other details of life and still manage to maintain such an amenable lifestyle?

And, for instance as well, the very nature of the relationship that intertwines their names, as literally represented by their business card, while still in no way defining their relationship. Are they perhaps friends? Or even relatives perhaps—immigrants from whatever nameless unknowable European nation from which Elsa gets her bewildering accent? Or lesbians, which would be the most logical relationship, given their ever-present presence in each other's lives and the size of their one bedroom cottage (if, indeed, they live there together—there was no proof that they did)?

But what about them might I conjecture?

Elsa: her soft, smooth face a mask. Her look, one of freshness, a woman of a certain age brave enough to wear no makeup, no jewels, only a simple, practical haircut that looked as if someone with scissors had traced a bowl. Albeit Tiffany scissors and a Lalique bowl.

She pitches her voice to a sigh. No, better: She pitches her voice lightly to sit on the air. With a whisper of a laugh. A harmonic laugh.

Emphasize later her love of pastels, how her complexion as well seems pastel as I think this is important: pink lips, light blue eyes, hair slightly silvered, yet likely considered blonde. She is petite in every way. Small body, petite spirit, as if her needs matched her wants, and each could fit in a walnut shell. Likely / not likely. Likely a small woman with outsized wants. Or so she seems.

House filled with shells. Conch. Others, as well, from oceans besides the Pacific. Found this telling.

Vera: Basso profundo to Elsa's piccolo. "Monster" (?)—question mark added due to the benefit of the doubt and the Grace of God. Voice of a lawnmower. Tits like a twenty-year-old, ass ripe and full. In between, a stick figure with a mass of peroxided hair on top. A mane of the old school—Farrah, Sharon Tate, Mamie Van Doren (!). Her face all ups and downs, hills and valleys, no planes. Elsa, on the other hand, is all planes, all soft and gentle edges. Vera has Mount Silicon on either side of her whittled nose. Sounds like a transplant from the Bronx who had her tongue shaved as well. But retains, oh, how she retains the viewpoint, the instinct, the capacity for criticism general and specific.

When I got down to the car, the two were busy looking side to side, as if debating with the driver the best route to our destinations. I tapped lightly on the window next to Elsa, who put her hand up to her throat in (mock?) apprehension before recognizing that it was I and not a panhandler or mobile psychic. She smiled then and opened the door. And insisted that she get out and allow me to sit between them.

"Oh, Jameson," she sighed in her sighing manner. "How grand you look."

"Someone's found his way back to himself," said the foghorn. We exchanged withering looks.

And off we went.

The clothing store, well, little need be reported about it. It was, indeed, a clothing store of the finest sort that was stocked with just the sort of things that one should own. And so now I do, a great many more than I did before, none of which are in any way sensible for a person living in the Northeast. All of them, however, seem to make perfect sense in the context of life here. I bought as if I were never going home. The boxes stacked up next to me as Elsa urged me on to more and more and Vera ran her hands over the goods as if she had ripped the fabric herself with her teeth and run them up on her sewing machine.

The driver took the boxes to the car. Those that would not fit in the trunk rode up front with him.

Next, we stopped briefly for cappuccinos, while the ladies took stock of me.

"This morning, I would have thought a chemical peel," brayed Vera, who took my face in her paws and twirled it from side to side. "But now he looks so much better."

No doubt from the steam and the scrub, I thought, but only shrugged at her.

"I think perhaps there will be a bit of filler here and here" said Elsa, poking at my eyes. "And if I know my dear Dr. Magellan, he will go with the hyaluronic acid. Masculane, I should think . . ."

"And I say the Prolactic," said Vera firmly. There was no doubt. There is never room for doubt when Vera speaks. "Sculptra is a much better filler for this sort of thing. It lasts so much longer and everything looks so much better in the long run."

"Yes, but, Vera, it also takes so much longer to work. No, Masculane, and he can walk out of the office today in a state of Grace."

"Well, Botox as well," said Vera, perhaps a bit cowed by Elsa's greater knowledge or perhaps not wanting to argue in Beverly Hills. She pointed her index finger to my neck and lightly traced what I suppose are rings. She pointed to my forehead as well.

"Of course! That's a given," said Elsa, her hand waving the air between them.

Elsa opened her purse and then pulled a small pink plastic case from within it. "Now Jameson," she sing-songed, "before you finish your coffee (she pronounced it 'caffe'), I want you to take one of these."

She put a small peach-colored pill in the palm of my hand, and closed my fingers around it.

"It's nothing, dear friend," she chirped. "It is only a Xanax to help calm you and ease your tension as we go into the doctor's office. It is very mild."

I considered debating the wisdom of taking any drug before going into the man's office but then complied. I simply plucked the pill out of her soft palm and popped it in my mouth and swallowed it dry. Only then did I sip my coffee, tasting the bitterness of the drug mixed with the bitterness of the drink.

I smiled the "all gone" smile I used to give to my mother or any of the step-doodles or her various toe-suckers and/or hangers-on when they told me to clean my plate.

"Ah, good," said Elsa.

"It's time we were going," said Vera, stating, as she often does, what is really completely obvious—she sees herself, I think as a Cassandra, when, in reality, she is only Margaret Mead working among a group of savages about which we already know more than we ought to.

I signaled for the bill and paid it. And we were off.

SEVENTEEN

*W*hich *puts us back in the car again, and me back sitting in the middle, staring at the back of the driver's neck. I hadn't really had much of a chance to take in anything else about him, but the back of his neck was pristine. Just everything that one might wish it to be. Perfectly clear of any errant hair; and his hairline in the rear was equally immaculate. Of the back of his head, I can only state that his hair was, like Chase's, black as night and wonderfully glossy. The head, I think, of a young Rock Hudson.*

It was the silent abyss into which I had slid, which largely featured trying to piece together the various components of the driver's face in the rear view without his notice that allowed me more or less to ignore the ongoing discussion of my flaws and of how Magellan was, apparently, putting himself to the gravest of tests in agreeing to treat me. I, apparently, had stage-four crow's- feet and needed to be seen and treated at the earliest possible interval.

And so.

And so.

Let me note that, while driving around Beverly Hills, more than once I considered the folly of my original destination and the possibility of simply picking up and moving myself into the pink luxury of the BH Hotel. But then, as we drove the immaculate streets, I came to realize that there was this secret about the place: it could have been anywhere. It was certainly luxurious. Hamptons luxurious. And certainly, in planning it and maintaining it, certainly the visionaries had stinted on nothing, and yet the highly manicured streets exhibited a certain soullessness, a certain lack of artistry that perhaps a few threads of crabgrass and a bit of dog poop might have added. But there it was. Iron-clad beauty, row after row of enormous mismatched houses, all with the same air of oxygen-free living. It showed there, as it did in the Orwellian shopping district in which we were now rather frantically searching for a parking space.

None found, it was decided by the ever-authoritarian Vera that Tony—for that was the name of our driver, who, when I finally got a good look at him, turned out to be the possessor of a pleasant, intelligent face (which is to say no beauty), and lucky enough to have rather exquisite azure blue eyes—would drop us at the entrance and then drive about until summoned on his cell phone.

As it turned out, the building where we were dropped looked as if it had been lifted whole from some rural village in the Cotswolds—a two-story affair combining fragile ancient brick and hearty ivy. The building was small and rather elegantly arranged on a corner, so that two small garden spaces, each teeming with annuals in vibrant colors, gleamed in the sunlight. They, like every other garden that I had seen since arriving, had the look of just having been watered, as beads of dew caused tiny explosions of pure, clear light as one walked past in the afternoon blaze.

I noticed as we passed that the sign on the door said only:

Balboa/Magellan
Second Floor

Nothing more. No mention of the honorifics. No days open, or hours present. Only names.

And nothing at all about the first floor, although that, too, had a door that opened onto the street. The downstairs looked quite possibly occupied, certainly well kept, and yet apparently something of a secret.

I mentioned the mysterious lack of information on the sign to Elsa, who replied, "And why should they, Jameson? Everyone who needs to know knows what they need to know already. Why complicate matters?"

To move on perhaps to the most pertinent part, let me state that, when I was finally in Dr. Magellan's chair, when the pain came it was of a less intrusive qual-ity than the pain Bucky had had to offer on that mad night that seemed weeks or months ago now, but it came with more frequency. And—and perhaps here my own bias comes into play, in that the sterile nature of Dr. Magellan's office would, for most people, be a thing of comfort, likely, and yet, for me, all such places, all such rooms of stainless steel, magnifying mirrors and spit sinks, are to be equated with blistering discomfort that, we are told again and again, is for our own benefit—so, it became a matter of whether one wants to be cut down in a single, searing blow, or die more slowly, the victim of a million little cuts.

And, oh, those million little cuts.
And, oh, from whose hands they came.

When one visits Dr. Magellan, one feels as if one is being presented to the queen.

I was ushered into a low-slung pleasure palace of a waiting room, with a wider array of beverages than the coffee store we had just left, all tucked above what Vera had finally explained to me was a ladies' boutique so exclusive that it had no name at all on the door, and was merely known by the first name of the woman who owned it, "Lisa."

Upstairs from Lisa, metal lamps hurtled themselves at me from every angle, assisted, no doubt, by that peachy little pill that Elsa had given me, which, in the few minutes since I took it, had begun to make me feel as if the car, the room, perhaps the entirety of the world, had shifted a bit and gotten a bit more uphill. Thus, my every step was something of an excursion in to some terra both incognita and infirma and the same steps involved more effort on my part, perhaps more conscious effort than I have been accustomed to requiring. Thus, thus, thus, I more or less paraded around the room, lifting my feet high with every step as if showing them my shoes.

I got up to the window and told the girl behind it, "I yam heeere to seeee Dr. Maygelleeeen."

I'm afraid, in spite of my best efforts, I may have slurred.

Vera and Elsa, who had, after all, made the call that had gotten me into this place (and only a call from one such as Elsa would have mattered, as I was to find out later when I was more or less told how very very lucky I should have felt to have been needled in this way) attempted to hide their faces in identical copies of Hello! Magazine—British edition.

And so I left my ladies, bid them adieu. I was taken into a small but elegantly appointed room, in which I was seated in a very comfortable chair. Next to me was a table with a disconcertingly large magnifying glass, an even more disruptive magnifying mirror, with lights encircling the reflective bit, several instruments of various degrees of sharpness, a plain drab denim-blue box of Kleenex and another equally comfortable looking chair.

I sat for a good while.

Quite suddenly, the door opened and a smiling man with an intriguing head of auburn hair (it seemed perhaps to be comprised of doll's hair) came into the room. His features in animation somehow suggested a rodent on his hind legs, in the way that many squinting young actors since Richard Gere have emulated the rodent. He had small eyes that were covered by horn-rimmed glasses and an open-collared shirt and slacks, over which he wore a white lab coat. Around his neck, as a likely affectation, he wore a stethoscope, that most unnecessary piece of medical equipment for all plastic surgeons.

Instead of sitting in the other chair, Magellan came right round, stuck out his hand and said to me, "Jameson Frame, it's good to meet you, you must call me Max," as he reached into his pocket, took out two translucent plastic gloves and inserted his hands into them. I assured him that I would and he perched on the table, allowing him to tower over me.

Pleasantries over, the doctor seized my head in his hands, spun the magnifying glass over in front of his eyes and looked at me, hard.

Several moments passed. There was a strange little humming in the air that I finally recognized as coming from the doctor himself. Finally Max spoke, while removing his plastic gloves.

"Well Jameson, as candidates go, you are rather ideal. I strongly suggest the injectables for you as the best course of treatment.

"In most cases like yours, with the onset of the fine laugh lines or crow's-feet," (he dangled his fingers in the air to suggest ironic uses of the words), "I most often use a wonderful new substance taken from polylactic acid named Sculptura, which enhances the body's own natural ability to make collagen, but as Elsa reports you are only with us for a limited time, I think the best course of treatment is instead one of the products taken from hyaluronic acid, which is another substance found naturally in the body, and therefore quite harmless. The product I suggest is called Masculane, which most of my gentleman clients prefer. It would be administered through injection," (he demonstrated this by allowing me to look into the mirror side of the glass as he grazed the outer corners of my eyes with his fingertip) "into these lines in the form of a gel. That gel becomes like a small pillow under the skin and supports tissue there, removing the lines and making the skin in the area seem younger and firmer."

At the mention of Masculane, I mentally awarded Elsa full points for precognition.

Max went on to mention that he would also prescribe Botox, as, apparently, Botox went quite well with Masculane. And as both are easily obtained and in global use, it was expected that any doctor of my own choice in Manhattan could manage my upkeep, as I would need to have more injections every three to four months to maintain full youth and vigor.

"How long will this treatment take?" I asked.

"Fifteen minutes or so," he said, putting his hand on my knee and lifting himself into a standing position. He looked at me for a moment, as if expecting me to speak.

"Shall we proceed?" he finally asked.

"Oh, yes, yes indeed," I answered in my peach haze.

"Good. I'll send the boy in."

"Boy?" I asked, suddenly seized by the possibilities.

"My physician's assistant. He will give you the actual injections. Under my supervision, of course."

"Of course."

Max Magellan started for the door, then remembered something and turned back.

"The Masculane works immediately. There may be a bit of swelling at the site of the injections, but usually there is nothing, and the lines are gone immediately. Botox will make a noticeable difference now, but will not show its full impact for three days."

Remembering my angry tattoo that was hidden from view and somewhat squelched from stinging by Elsa's Xanax, I began to ask a question about it, but Max raised a benign palm and continued, "You'll be twenty years younger by dinner tonight," he said, smiling, and then he was gone.

Alone in the room once more, I looked into the reflective magnifying mirror, and with a sudden sense of horror, I tore at the dry, brittle skin around my eyes. Perhaps this was stage four after all, I thought. Perhaps we have gotten here just in time. And I admit that, alone in that room, in that moment in Beverly Hills, California, I studied my face like Norma Desmond.

There was a sudden sharp rap on the door.

It flew open to admit a tall and very handsome young man with a mane of bright yellow hair, who pushed the door open with his hip. In his hands, there was a wide tray of needles, various bottles filled with various things and other instruments of torture, all covered with a single, perfectly laundered white towel. The young man set the tray on the table in front of me. As he did so, he, like the doctor, perched on the corner of the table, once more towering over me. I looked up to see his ruddy face bracketing a wide, glossy smile.

"Mr. Frame, I don't believe you remember me," he said.

Staring at his thorax, I admitted that he had me at a disadvantage.

"Actually, I am glad you didn't remember me, Mr. Frame, because when we met before, I was rather rude. You see, I was very tired, so when we got on the plane from New York, I was determined to get some sleep. It wasn't until we got back here to Los Angeles that Toby told me who you were. Naturally I was bitterly disappointed that I hadn't had the chance to shake hands with my favorite poet.

"You remember me now, right? Kyle?"

And he extended a large hand toward me, as if he were enacting the role of Myles Standish in an elementary school's Thanksgiving pageant.

"I hope we can meet now as if for the first time."

We shook. I smiled and said how nice it was that fate had given us a second chance to meet.

"I couldn't believe it yesterday when I answered the phone and Elsa asked if we could squeeze you in. When she said your name, I just thought of how Toby was going to take the news if I had said that we were booked up for two months in advance, and so I said, by all means, bring him in for a nooner."

Kyle came around the table and took the cloth off the tray. I admit I blanched as he prepared several needles with the injectable gel. While he worked, he said, "Toby has done nothing but talk about you since the two of you talked on the plane. He usually isn't so excited about meeting celebrities, we have so many of our own here, but he is always impressed by men of letters." He jingled his masculine eyebrows at me as he spoke.

He then swabbed my face as he was saying that, when he had told Toby about my appointment today, Toby had insisted that he invite me to their home for dinner tonight, no doubt so that the two of us could have a chance to reminisce about our plane ride together.

As he leaned over me, I noticed that the necklace he wore slipped free, exposing a glittery letter K, as well as a few tufts of wheat-colored hair.

As he jabbed me for the first time, right next to my right eye, which caused me to see blue pinwheels of sparks in that eye and to cry out with a shrill "Eek," he asked me if I had any food allergies or if there was anything that I particularly disliked when it was presented to me on a plate. I assured him that I was not a difficult eater and that I tried at all times to be a pleasant guest, before I returned my fist to my mouth in order to bite down during the second injection.

By the time the right eye (five injections in total!) was finished and the needles were prepped for my left eye, I had agreed to dine with them that evening.

How could I not?

How could I deny anything to anyone who was, in that moment, needling so very near my eye?

Every time I saw the needle move into my line of vision, move closer closer slowly slowly I knew in my heart that, had I had the secrets of World War II locked in my mind, and had I been captured, that Hitler very likely would have won the war. In my mind's eye, Kyle was suddenly the perfect Aryan, with his blond hair, needles and perfect teeth.

At last he finished.

I was instructed not to touch my eyes for a period of time and to watch them for the next three days, as nodules sometimes formed at the area of the injection and reactions to the Botox were not unknown.

Before he could run from the room, I put my hand on his, looked pleadingly into his eyes, and asked him rather nicely if he would be willing to look at a wound that I had that was causing me some trouble.

Lifting my leg, he said, "It's a V, a perfect little V," before swabbing it, frowning at it, and telling me to keep an eye on it, before wrapping it in gauze. He put a small container of rub into a small white paper bag, folded the top over and handed it to me.

"This should take care of it," he said, not unkindly. "Looking forward to tonight."

I left the inner office with my leg feeling much better, but with a new sense of angry redness and a stinging headache in both my temples. In spite of the peach Xanax, a certain sense of irritability settled over me, most conclusively when I thought to ask Kyle for his address.

Giving me his card, he said, "You won't need this. Elsa can just give the address to your driver. Likely, she already has."

To which I replied, "Uh, uuummphhh."

"We'll see you at eight, then," Kyle said, waving me out the door and over toward the front desk, where I was presented with a sizable bill.

"Yes, eight. Good," I said, casting the best smile that I could over to Vera, who looked over at me from where she sat on the couch and Elsa, who stood, looking my way anxiously and mouthing, "Does it hurt?" while she pulled at her own eyes in a vaguely Asian manner.

EIGHTEEN

∽

That night, the sun fitted the sky in a scarlet bandeau, which blended into darkness as Frame watched from his hotel room, preparing for his evening out. He felt a clutch of melancholy in his chest as day faded. He thought for a moment of his cabin, of the coals in the fireplace and how they glowed the same scarlet at evening's end, when darkness had hunched around the cabin for hours, preparing him sweetly for the night.

Here, darkness came too early. And offered no slow embers. Only a gyrating sense of aloneness that Frame had never quite grasped before.

In that moment, he imagined again the tumult of the deep waters facing him, felt, like Ophelia, her sense of being caught up, swept under, her feeling of being weighted down by the finery that life had provided, and his own dread of the weight that his own life brought him. He put his hand up to the glass of the great glittery pane in front of him, pressed his toes into the glass and looked as directly down as he could, to comfort himself with the playtime ongoing on the boardwalk.

Suddenly that narrow walkway and the filthy patch of sand seemed such insignificant barriers against the water. He pushed himself back, leaving the smudge of his handprint perfectly visible on the glass.

He went to his dresser and selected cufflinks, threaded them, handled neckties, rejected them and stood in front of his mirror, a well-dressed man in more of the many new clothes that he had just bought.

Steeled against the night in Armani armor, he left the room, the hotel, and seated himself again in the back seat of Anthony's town car.

In the back seat, Frame found the small box with the ornate silk ribbon that he had asked be picked up from a nearby bakery, to be offered as a gift to his hosts. He treasured the box in his hands, feeling the soft weight of it in his lap as they drove.

Here, he reasoned, he could lower himself into shadows, enjoy the stentorian lights all around him, the promises sworn in flashing, multi-colored bulbs, the gigantic light-painted billboards, and the searchlights that seemed as inevitable here as oranges and lemons; all would bring his heart to rest again.

The light faded as they made their meandering way down Sunset, allowing Frame to delight in the neon dawn. The sun was quite gone by their turn onto Doheny. Upward they went, Anthony quick on the steering wheel, tossing them to the left and then to the right as they climbed the narrow, steep roadway into the hills.

Soon they were enveloped in a maze of avian names: Bluebird, Blue Jay, Oriole, and the street they turned on, Nightingale. Quickly pulling over after the narrow turn to let another car pass in the opposite direction, Anthony smoothed their path forward, careened around another curve and pulled to a stop in front of a small, very modern looking home. The house was comprised of boxes, two side-by-side with another up on top. The front was cantilevered away from the others. All were composed largely of glass and light spilled out from the house, as did heavily pulsating music.

Frame pushed his door open before Anthony could stop the engine. He stepped out of the car and stood staring at the house. Inside, he could see a figure rushing about, moving first to the rear of the house, waving his arms as he went, and then to the side and then to the front, where the door flew open, silhouetting the figure against the light that spilled forth, illuminating Frame's face.

"Jameson Frame!" shouted a small, spry figure.

The Ghoul, thought Frame, who said, merely, "How nice to see you, Toby, and how nice of you and Kyle to have me over for dinner."

At that moment, Anthony backed the long town car into the driveway, separating the two men, and drove off in the direction of the Sunset Strip.

"I told him to come back for me at ten," said Jameson Frame, stretching out his hand, offering his ribbon-wrapped box to the Ghoul. "I hope that was all right."

"Entirely too early," replied the Ghoul, ignoring the offering for a moment and embracing him instead. "But come in, come in."

As he passed through the doorway, Frame again resisted the urge to scratch the skin around his eyes. He had been resisting just this inclination for the better part of two hours. While preparing himself for this evening, he had looked at his face in the mirror, eager to see the miraculous loss of a human generation in just a quarter hour and wondering in spite of himself if it would be something that Chase would ever notice, that would even matter to him.

When he looked in the mirror, he saw to his amazement that, no matter how he might struggle to create lines in his face—contorting his face in apparent mirth one moment, looking fretful the next and quite wickedly wanton in a third attempt at crinkly emotion—he could not do so. The face in the mirror remained a calm, smooth plane. As he drew closer to the mirror however, and turned his head to see the outer portion of his cheeks and upward to his eyes, he saw, to his horror, the presence of a group of small, red, angry wens at the site of the injections. It was these that itched and, with their discoloration, called themselves to the attention of anyone looking at Frame's face far more than any laugh lines could.

Even the Ghoul, whose own face was a powdery dry white vague interpretation of the mask of humanity, one of indeterminate age and gender, thanks no doubt to the ministry of Drs. Balboa and Magellan, noticed.

"Oh, before we go in, stand right here in the good light and let me see the work you had done. I cannot wait to see it!"

The Ghoul, not quite daring to touch the face of Jameson Frame instead pulled himself up onto his toes in order to study quite clearly the outcome of Kyle's injections. He lifted his hands to within inches of Frame's jawline, and cradled it, looking hard.

"Oh, dear," he said, almost inaudibly, and he took the box from Frame's hands.

"Huh?" Frame asked, suddenly feeling as if his knees would give way.

"It's quite good, Jameson," said the Ghoul comfortingly, walking around a pony wall into the open kitchen area, putting the box on the counter, fluffing the ribbon and walking back again to lean toward Frame over the pony wall. "The Masculane has filled the lines perfectly, with a million little pillows supporting the furrows from within. Just perfect. It's just that—"

"Good evening, Mr. Frame," said Kyle, entering the room wearing only a towel. His hair was wet, and his ripped chest shed the downward flowing water into rivulets. He pulled off his towel and used it to dry his hair. Beneath it he wore a bright red Speedo.

"Forgive me, I wanted to get a quick swim in before dinner," he said unapologetically. "Let me just get changed—"

"Kyle," said the Ghoul with some urgency. "Take a look at this."

He came over and stood between the two of them. He took Frame's head in his massive hands and turned the site of the injections to the light. He touched the wens with the tip of his finger, sending shocks along the nerves in Frame's teeth.

"Ah," said Kyle, sounding like Dr. Magellan. "These nodules are quite common. They are really a slight allergic reaction and will disappear all on their own. Be careful not to scratch or irritate them, Mr. Frame, and they will clear up on their own. If they cause you any real discomfort or if they don't clear up soon, just come back into the office and we can treat them."

"How long do they usually last?"

"Well, not more than three months at most. Usually less time than that, several weeks at most."

"But isn't that the amount of time the injection lasts?" Frame asked somewhat tersely.

"You'll be fine," said Kyle, snapping the top of his swimming trunks. "I want to get changed now," his eyes and his gilt K both glittering.

And Kyle disappeared into the adjoining cube of the house, while the Ghoul slipped his arm into Frame's and steered him into the living room, where the lights had been lowered to emphasize the view.

Frame stopped in his tracks. In front of him lay Los Angeles in panorama, with a view sweeping from downtown on his left to the ocean far to his right. The Ghoul urged him forward, took him through a French door to the deck beyond, from where the view was more staggering still, the city lights that had been dulled by the reflective glass were now more pronounced than stars in the night sky.

"It's called a 'jetliner view,' Jameson. All the way from sunrise over downtown," he gestured with his left hand, "to sunset over the Pacific on the right."

Frame watched transfixed as the traffic snaked through the dark lawn of the cityscape; he was riveted by the madcap lights, the neons, the billboards, the searchlights, the twinkle of lights turned on, the sudden loss of lights turned off.

Kyle quietly joined them on the terrace. He came up behind the Ghoul and embraced him, putting his scruffy chin on the older man's shoulder, slipping a glass of cold white wine into the man's hand. The Ghoul pressed himself into the younger man's form, resting within it; he took a slow, satisfied sip of his wine. Kyle lifted his left arm and placed a hand in the center of Frame's back as well, joining the three briefly as a unit. Then he dropped his hand and they stood, speckled in lights from a million sources, a million colors.

"Let us go then," said Frame quietly. *"You and I,*

"When the evening is spread out against the sky

"Like a patient etherized upon a table."

"Jameson, you baptized our home with poetry."

"Ah, but not mine, alas," he said to the Ghoul, "Eliot's."

"Let me get you some wine, Mr. Frame," said the youth, moving away from the men and to the French doors.

"Dusty In Memphis" was playing from a hidden sound system, the speakers of which had been embedded into the framework of the house in such a way that sound bathed them from all directions at the same time.

"You remember Dusty, don't you Jameson?" asked the Ghoul, shoving a small stick-like arm into Frame's rib. "All of us do!" The "us" seemingly a reference both to age and to sexual identity.

"Ah, I think of her with that hair piled up to here," he said, raising an arm high above his head. "She was a Lez, you know, but such a voice, such a voice."

They were seated around a round Charles Eames table on which a minimalist dinner of grilled vegetables and sushi had been placed by unseen hands.

After an evening of raw foods and rich music from his favorite girl singers—Streisand, Rosemary Clooney, whom he called "Rosey" in his ongoing aria of memories, Bernadette Peters, Elaine Stritch ("Stritchy") and the like—the Ghoul became rather effusive on the subjects of music and the harrowing tales of gay life when Judy Garland's Carnegie Hall was later played from what the Ghoul insisted was a rare master recording.

During her rendition of "The Man That Got Away," after several glasses of a rather nice Cabernet Sauvignon, the Ghoul had himself burst into song in his own waspish Katharine Hepburny voice. Kyle ululated as the Ghoul mimed throwing flowers into the crowd and told tales of who had and had not been in the audience that night, no matter what they told you.

He then became even more animated on the subject of the Last Days of Judy, whose life, he noted, had been one of tragedy—bad romances and a failed career. The latter part brought tears to his eyes, as Frame fiddled with his chopsticks.

"I was but a baby then, of course," the Ghoul whispered through his tears.

What brought Frame's eyes back to attention was the tableau of Kyle bending over to the Ghoul and kissing him, hard, full on the lips. The corpse wrapped his arms around the younger man, who seemingly offered his friend the full measure of his youth and animus. An electrical current flew between the two of them as they remained intertwined. The old man arose to stand with the boy like figures on a wedding cake.

When at last the two released each other, Kyle slumped back in his Eames chair, his half-closed eyes on Jameson Frame, a sly smile on his face. He raised the back of his hands to his mouth and wiped it.

The Ghoul's eyes rested on Kyle, shifting ever so slightly from side to side, seeing his yellow hair, his broad forehead, heavy brow, blue eyes, full lips, and rough chin. Resting now, calm now, he returned to his chair and looked away into the city night.

And the music played on, one song after the next. Several times throughout that evening Kyle had had to remind Frame not to touch the bumps that itched so.

At ten o'clock, Frame climbed back in his car, over the protests of his hosts, who stood in their doorway, side-by-side, arm in arm. He feigned regret, waved and sat back in the darkness, pressing and holding the button to raise the window against the night.

His head ached with a deep, dull throb. The skin around his eyes burned, as did his eyes. He wanted only darkness then, only stillness and darkness and silence. And some of the baked goods that he himself had brought, but were never served during the whole of the dessertless evening.

Anthony, who had been quietly listening to talk radio, turned it down and then off with a soft click. He drove cautiously down from the hills and ultimately rejoined the river of traffic on Sunset. Together, they drove without speaking, the driver intent on his work, the passenger again bringing Prufrock into his field of vision, writ large and cursive over Sunset Boulevard:

> Let us go then, you and I,
> When the evening is spread out against the sky
> Like a patient etherized upon a table;
> Let us go, through certain half-deserted streets,
>
> The muttering retreats
>
> Of restless nights in one-night cheap hotels
> And sawdust restaurants with oyster-shells:
> Streets that follow like a tedious argument
>
> Of insidious intent
>
> To lead you to an overwhelming question. . . .
> Oh, do not ask, "What is it?"
> Let us go and make our visit.

"I have come," said Jameson Frame to the yellow neon pinwheel of a liquor store sign from which the "I" had long ago burned and fallen, leaving him stopped at the red light under the jaundiced light of the "L quor Store" sign, "I am here at last on my visit."

NINETEEN

⁓

Best to leave the lights off, he thought as he came back into his suite. *Best to*, he began again, reasoning with himself as one would with an irascible child, and then, losing the thought, as he again resisted the urge to scratch the skin around his eyes, or the patch on his left leg that was throbbing so. Suddenly, he dropped his trousers to the floor, stepped out of them, ripped the gauze off his left leg and scratched long and hard. The voluptuous feel of it. A dog would, in feeling such rapture, helplessly kick his other leg up and down, up and down, pounding the floor in his glee.

Frame wrapped his body around the knee of that leg and hissed as the pain returned, intensified from the raking of his nails. Hissed again as he raised himself up, walked over to the bar, and attempted to pour himself a healthy drink. Stymied by the dark, he put on a light, but then, faced with the sight of his red eyes, and the angry wens around them, he fetched his sunglasses and placed them on his face with a "humphhh" before returning to the bar.

He put ice in the bottom of the glass and then several slugs of good whiskey. He swirled the liquid, its amber beauty intensified by the tint of his lenses. Double amber, the liquid looked magical, transformative. He tipped his index finger into it, rubbed droplets on the ridge of his upper teeth and then took a long, soothing drink. He felt the strength of it blast against the back of his throat, sucked down a cough and drank again.

Again, he dipped his finger into the glass, this time rubbing it against the angry V on his left leg. The pain again intensified, forcing him to hop a step or two on his right leg as he issued a single, clipped "fuck." He stood, as best he could, his shirt loose, his striped silk boxers comfortably hanging and his sunglasses sliding down the length of his nose.

"Fuck," he said again.

And again and again and again.

He made and drank another drink, walked over to the desk, turned on the lamp and reached for the computer's switch. Turning it on as well, he felt the machine purr with life. He stood before it as the screen began to glow.

Standing there, he thought again of what he had pondered and deconstructed all during his ride home. The thing had haunted him, even as he thanked Anthony for his skill and trouble, over-tipping him for his long day's work. The thing that he saw in his mind's eye as the town car disappeared in the distance.

The image of the Ghoul's dry tongue disappearing into the warm, wet mouth of his young friend.

How many times, he wondered, had the young man had to stifle the crone with the promises implied in such a deep kiss? Promises of fidelity against the maw of age, of a warm, furry body in one's own California King-sized bed? And what was the cost of such kisses?

On the screen in front of him, again under the title of "The Waters of Venice," he wrote it down, standing up and hunching over while typing, his sloppy wet glass ringing the fine burled wood surface of the desk:

What is the cost of such kisses?

In celebration of such insightful work, he wandered back to the bar leaving his old glass where it was, finding a new, shiny one, and opened another of the little bottles of very nice whiskey, ignored the cost, and poured. He held the cool glass against each of his throbbing eyes and against the now volcanic pain of his left calf.

Refuting the need for a return to the computer keyboard, he went instead into the bedroom, and threw himself down on the bed, lying on his back, his right arm across his forehead, the glass resting on his chest. He felt his heart under the glass, pumping up against it, not coming to rest as his body did, but pounding fiercely, as if it would surely burst.

He felt the bed, the room twist around him and wondered: *Is it the room moving, or am I?* He pondered this so deeply, feeling his heart questioning itself from within his chest, that he almost did not hear the rap at his door.

"Ah," he said, and "fuck" once again. He thrust his glass straight up in the air and attempted to bring his body after, but could not. Instead, he twisted his body so that his knees fell to the floor and then pushed himself erect, his glass tucked in at his side. He shook the ice in the glass and sipped once, twice, while making his way to the door.

He saw the trousers where he left them and kicked at them to keep them from interfering with the opening of the door, put his hand on the handle and opened it.

In front of him, all jagged with perhaps the energy of youth and no doubt augmented by some artificial source was Chase, whose eyes lit up with a smile when they saw him, with his mouth forming a grin soon after.

"Jimmy," he said with his cupid bow of a mouth, forming the words as if loosing an arrow. "Can I come in?"

Jameson Frame, without hesitation, threw the door fully open, tangling it in the dropped trousers and stepped back to allow the youth to enter the suite.

"What's with the glasses?" he asked as he walked in. "Incognito?"

Frame woofed a laugh and watched the youth stride into and about the room, watched the way his body moved in space. He pulled at the door and then at the trousers, tossing them aside again, and heard the click of the lock.

"Chase," he said, using the only word he could muster. "Chase." Meaning all things with that one word.

"I was here earlier, but you didn't answer. You had me worried, Jimmy. I thought maybe you were gone," he said, looking up at Frame from the couch. "So I checked at the desk and they said you were still here, so I got a burrito. You want some?"

He took a large wrapped object out of a bag and put it down on the coffee table in front of him. He took a six-pack that was missing a can out of the bottom of the bag and wadded the bag up and dropped it to the floor.

Frame shook his head no. Chase unwrapped the end of the package and took a bite. "It's good," he said in a muffled manner, his mouth filled with meat, beans and cheese. He held the burrito out in front of him.

Remembering the stilted dinner, the large plates with small servings of sushi and vegetables, Frame suddenly felt hungry, took the food from the youth and, laughing, took a large bite.

"It is good!" he said, his own mouth filled to overflowing.

Frame managed to seat himself on the floor and they passed the burrito back and forth, finishing it and each finishing a beer as well.

Frame got up off the floor after eating and made his way to the bar again, opening another small bottle of whiskey. He held a bottle out to the boy, who shook his head, held up one of his own beers, and then opened it. The older man put fresh ice in his glass and drained the bottle into it, licking the tip of the bottle after pouring.

He walked over and sat down on the couch with Chase, looked at the boy, who was dressed in his inevitable shorts, sleeveless striped T and scuffed white athletic shoes, wishing for it all to fall away.

Chase looked at him again and said, "The glasses," as if listing unfinished business. And he reached over and took the glasses from Frame's face.

"Oh, dude," he said with regret, shaking his head slowly. His eyes grew moist. "Why'd you let them stick you with that stuff?" he asked.

Frame felt the whole of his face redden, felt heat run through the whole of his being. Hiding behind the crystal glass he held tight in front of his tumbling heart, his only response was to shake his head. He felt his own eyes water at the thought of what had been done to them.

Chase narrowed his eyes and brought his face close. He watched the formation of a tear in the older man's right eye, and, when the droplet of water began its path down the side of his face, the boy soothed it away with a fingertip. "Ah, Jimmy," he said. "What are we going to do with Jimmy?" he asked the thin air, speaking very clearly, biting off every word. He leaned back on the couch and thought for a moment. He folded his hands behind his head. "You know," he said, staring straight forward, "if you were going to do anything, maybe you should have had a little lipo and, you know, sucked away that belly you've got."

Frame's hand went to his stomach, pressing it from over his shirt.

Seeing the involuntary gesture, Chase laughed lightly and brought his own two hands up under Frame's shirt, resting one palm on either side of the man's stomach. "Don't get me wrong, Jimmy," he said, "I like your little belly. I just meant, if you were going to have something done, you might want to start there. I mean, it's just like the injectables, you get it done at lunchtime. In and out."

Frame winced at the contact of Chase's hands on his body, but did nothing to prevent it. In fact, he leaned his body ever so slightly so that he rested in Chase's hot hands hidden under the folds of his shirt.

The boy responded to Frame's motion by slipping his hands up further, sliding them across the smooth skin of Frame's back, fully embracing him. And, as they drew close, he rested his head against Frame's shoulder and then brought his face down until he nuzzled the older man's chest.

In the moment, against all his yearnings, all Frame could think of quite suddenly was the Ghoul and his boy and the dry tongue on the lush wet carpet of the boy's mouth. And, with his back to them, he saw the words that were blinking still on the screen of the computer: *What is the cost of such kisses?* And he felt in that moment that there was no cost so high that he would not pay it, would not willingly give it for this boy, this perfect youth. He felt the scratch of the boy's scruff through the soft fabric of his shirt, felt the heat of his breath. And felt the sensations of his own body, his heartbeat now wild, erratic, the pains inside of him, physical mental emotional, the need to both pull this one near and push him away, the need to taste him.

Slowly, the boy unwound his arms, drew back his touch, a promise seemingly offered, instead withheld. "Uh, Jimmy," the boy said, smoothing his face upward so that his lips brushed against Frame's quivering Adam's apple. "I came here to find you tonight," he continued, sitting up and facing Frame and then reaching one hand into his own shirt to scratch himself right on his nipple. Looking down, Frame noticed, through the armhole of the sleeveless shirt, that the nipple that night wore a piercing. "Because I need your help with something," the boy said, his eyes wide, his hands in his lap like a supplicant. "Can I count on you, Jimmy?" he asked. "Will you help me?"

TWENTY

∽

"**S**ay you'll help me, Jimmy," the youth said as he fished first in the right pocket of his shorts and then in the left. "I want you to help me make art," he said, making the word "art" sound somehow both vile and thrilling. He pulled forth from his pants a small metal device and handed it to Frame.

The older man fumbled with the thing, not sure what it was or how to use it. Chase took it from him, pressed a button, flipped a small screen and showed him the video camera. He put it back into Frame's hands.

"Just look through here," he said.

As Jameson Frame held the camera up and looked into the view-finder, trying to point the lens at Chase, the boy stood up and walked into the bedroom. From the sitting room, Frame could see the lights go on, one, two three, and those on the cornices on the walls slowly flare up on their dimmer. The room was aglow as Frame walked into it.

The boy was lying on the bed, with one foot lifted up to the ceiling, and the shoe he had just removed from that foot lingering in his hands, as he tossed it lightly like a basketball dribbling in the cool air. He finally tossed the shoe to the floor, grabbed at the other and tossed it as well. His filthy feet looked a different color from the rest of his pale skin. Both feet bare, he rested his legs wide on the bed. Laughing, he made a snow angel in the deep pile of the coverlet, bunching the fabric around him in a swirl.

"Come on, Jimmy. It'd be so great. I needed a place to tape this and then I remembered this from the other night and it just seemed so right." He bounced up on his hands and knees, face pointed at Frame. "Dude, you just got to say yes…" and he rolled his eyes at the older man and sat back on his haunches, reaching his hands out, imploringly.

Frame, feeling the moment of possibility recede with each second of silence on his part, suddenly blurted a fervent "Yes," making both himself and the younger man laugh. "I mean, I'll do my best," said Frame.

"Jimmy, we're gonna make some art!" the boy crowed. And he reached in his pants and brought out a fat hand-rolled cigarette and a pack of restaurant matches, both of which came from a sandwich bag in his pocket, still quite full of joints.

Before Frame could protest, the boy said, "This comes first. It helps the art." He struck a match to the cigarette and inhaled deeply.

Frame, suddenly nervous that the smell of the thing would reach the hallway, quickly closed the bedroom door. Seeing this, the boy sputtered with laughter and issued a cloud of smoke that obscured his face.

"Man, Jimmy. I mean, man!" he cried, snorting. Then he patted the floor next to him and said, "Come here."

Frame sat on the floor next to the boy, feeling achy enough throughout his body that he had no intention of refusing the smoke. He inhaled as deeply as he dared and found that he was able to hold the smoke down without choking. He continued to hold his breath, looking at his feet.

Finally Chase said, "Breathe, Jimmy," and the older man exhaled with a loud cough. He took another drag on the joint before returning it to Chase.

"It doesn't take much, Jimmy. You don't have to work so hard."

"I can remember doing this a hundred years ago," Frame said, allowing his head to slide down the bed a bit to rest on the fleshy part of Chase's arm.

"Yeah?" said Chase with genuine surprise. He looked at the older man with something like respect. "Well, it's a lot stronger now. You really only need a hit or two," Chase said as Frame again took possession of the joint. "That's it now," Chase said as Frame inhaled deeply, the joint held between his thumb and index finger with his palm curled under. The boy took back the joint and let it rest on his lower lip as he got up, and searched for something he could use to snuff it out. He flattened it against the keycard that Frame had thrown on the dresser. Then he put the joint back into the baggy he had in his pants pocket.

His shoulder support removed, Frame had fallen to the floor, where he laid on the thick carpet, curled on his side. From there, he watched

Chase again as he moved about the room, considering the flow of the muscles in his body to be something richly, tenderly miraculous.

"You okay, Jimmy?" Chase asked the grinning man. "Fuck. I hope so." And he squatted and lifted Frame's dead weight, resting him against the bed again. He held the man's face in his hands, stared into his eyes and shook the older man's head again and again. Frame grinned at him and opened his mouth wide with a smile.

Chase reached down and pressed hard on the V on the inside calf of the man's left leg.

Frame let out a startled cry and sat bolt upright, shoving the boy to the floor as he rose.

"Fuck," said Frame, wincing in pain.

"Fuck, Jimmy," said Chase, laughing. "We better make us some art!"

He got up and went into the sitting room, only to return moments later with Frame's shiny laptop. He sat down on the floor again next to Frame, who, cunningly, brought his head once more slowly, slowly, down the side of the bed until his lips this time touched the meat of Chase's arm. He kissed his bicep softly, hoping the boy would not pull away.

Chase gave a vague wave in the air, as if a mosquito were annoying him. His fingers flew on the keyboard. His website appeared and he moved the cursor down the left side of the page, pointed to a link labeled "Secret Sanctuary" and pressed it. Another page appeared. At the top was a picture of Chase quite nude trussed up against a tree in the outdoors. His arms were tied up over his head. The position of his body suggested a saint, suffering. Peter. Sebastian. His disposition was of one brought to ecstasy through suffering. His long, heavy penis swayed between his legs.

Frame read what he could of the words on the page without moving his head from Chase's arm.

"See, Jimmy, this is the part of the site that guys pay to belong to. And we stay in touch, you know? They email me and suggest some things and if I want to do it, I do, but after telling them what the price is."

He moved the cursor over a button.

"See, I take PayPal."

"So, you make art to order?"

"Yeah, Jimmy, yeah. It's all art to order. That's what makes it special. It's like a private conversation between them and me. They tell me what they want to see and, if it feels right, if I like the guys, I show them.

"Sometimes it's like I can feel them wanting.

"And sometimes I hold an auction with some of the stuff from my shoots. Props. Underwear. Long johns. And they get to say whether they want me to wash it first or not. It's extra if I don't."

The boy laughed.

"And tonight?"

"Some of the Chasers wanted me to make a jerk-off video and I thought it'd be great if I could make it with me in a really nice bed."

"And why not have Mikey help you."

"Mikey gets kind of upset with this stuff. It's weird having him in the room when I'm making my art, you know," he said in the voice of a child.

"So Mikey stayed home?"

"Yeah, but I thought about you and about this room and being in your bed and I wanted to make this art with you, Jimmy."

"That's nice. I'm happy that you thought of me," Frame said, strangely moved at the idea.

"So, okay?" asked Chase.

"Yeah," said Frame, "okay."

"Fuck, yeah," said Chase, extending his hand for Frame to shake. When the older man took it, the younger pulled him into a tight embrace, smacking his back with his free hand.

"Fuck," said Frame, out of breath from the grip. "Yeah," he sighed, melting into the embrace.

Remembering the boy's feet in the air, Frame said, "Well the first thing you really want to do is take a good hot shower, scrub yourself clean."

"Hey, great man, we'll start in the shower," said Chase as he walked to the bathroom, tossing first his shirt and then his shorts into the air behind him.

When Frame got the camera up and running, Chase was already standing under a steady stream of water.

"Keep an eye out it doesn't get too hot," Chase told him. "If there's too much steam it will ruin the shot. So we want just enough. Keep the bathroom door open just a little and open and close it to control the steam."

Frame looked at the boy. He stood in the shower quite perfectly, with his head and face tipped forward enough to keep his hair dry.

"Are you running yet?"

"Yeah," said Frame. "Go ahead."

As he attempted to follow the action with the camera, Chase lowered his white briefs and soaked them in the streaming water. He tugged the front of his briefs down to expose the base of his penis and a small mound of dark hair that flowed out from the trail of hair above. He stuck his hand down into his briefs, grasping himself, and looking directly into the camera.

Frame kept the camera locked onto the boy's crotch.

"No, Jimmy," said Chase angrily. He turned off the water and stepped out of the shower, letting his briefs snap back up into place.

"Look, Jimmy, you have to tell a story with the camera." He held out his hand for it and took the camera away from Frame. "You have to move it, let it run smooth against my skin," he said, pointing the camera lens at his own leg and slowly pulling it up the length of it, filming each muscle as he slowly shifted them to best effect. "You just let it rest a bit on my dick, but then you have to move on. They want to see my face. They think they only want to see my cock, but they really want to see my face."

"You have to do some shots where you pull out and some where you push in," he said, now moving the lens in toward his foot again until it rested in a tight shot.

"You have to do all that so that I'll have something to edit later. You can't just stare at my cock the whole time. Where's the art in that?"

With that, Chase shoved the camera back into Frame's hands and stepped back into the shower.

This time, Frame started with Chase's face; he focused the camera on a pout in his eyes that his lips soon copied. And the boy slowly, beauti-ulled his head under the spray of the shower, keeping his face per-nd erect, then allowing his face to register first a quiet hunger and then a vague amusement. With each breath, the boy's face shifted again, giving a new emotion, expressing an internalized sexual thrill.

As his hands moved to the briefs once more, Frame instinctively moved the camera down across the wiry hair of the boy's chest, until the mountain range of his abdominals appeared in tight focus. Again the boy played with himself, jostled his cock for the camera, exposed his balls. And Frame pictured there a cut to his face, to an expression of secret thrill and began to understand better the art of filmmaking.

This segment done, Chase lowered his body slowly, keeping his legs long and muscular for the shot and then pulled off his briefs, wringing them out with a laugh, and hung them on the rod of the shower, while moving his body again under the rain of the shower, letting a thousand threads of water play down his body.

He showed flank to the camera, and ass. He took Frame's loofah down and soaped it with Frame's goat-milk soap and rubbed it hard across his skin. He covered his hair and face with suds and rinsed them away, spitting a fountain of water from his pink lips, which Frame caught in a beautiful close shot.

At last, he turned off the water and stepped out of the shower and languorously dried himself with the hotel's deeply plush bath sheet, bringing a pink glow to his porcelain skin.

He gathered the towel loosely at his waist and looked at Frame. He made an "okay" sign with his fingers and said, "All right, Jimmy, let's see what we got."

He took the camera and, walking into the bedroom once more, attached it with a cord from his shorts pocket to the laptop.

He stood there, damp, towel at his waist, watching the video and tutting from time to time over the camera work.

Frame stood behind him, unbearably close, inhaling him as he watched the screen, finding it impossible to believe that the man in the video stood nearly nude so very close, so easily to be touched.

Chase set the computer down and turned to him. His lips smiled, his eyes hard in appraisal.

After a second, the warmth returned to his face.

"You did really well, Jimmy," he finally said. "Man, I knew you could do it, and, dude, you sure as fuck did it." He slapped Frame on the shoulder.

"Now, we're going to start with the camera in this room, aimed at the bathroom door, which is ajar. I'll come out with the towel on, and drop it just as I pass the camera and you're shooting me from behind. So make sure to play down enough to get my ass in the shot. Not tight on my ass, but my ass is the star of the shot.

"Then we're going to get me on the bed. I lean over it and climb up on one knee. That's when you can get a great shot of my ass and my balls from behind. Then I'll roll over onto my back and, now that we got all the preliminary stuff, we can get to the main event."

"Yeah?" asked Frame, dry-mouthed.

"It's a jerk-off video, dude. Just do what you did in the shower, it was great," he said, hitching up the towel a bit. "Face and dick—that's what they all want, with long, slow crawls all over my body, like their hands were all over me.

"And whatever you do, don't miss my cum shot."

TWENTY-ONE

✎

When they were done recording, Jameson Frame, wobbly though he might be, displayed proudly his own erection, which shot forth from the opening in his boxers. He put the camera aside and looked at Chase, instead of squinting through the camera's undersized viewfinder. The youth, who lay supine on the California King, said, "Don't I get a towel? Dude, I need a towel."

And Frame went into the bathroom to fetch one, so that he might wipe the boy's hand and dab away at the streaks of semen that covered his chest.

"Did we miss any, Jimmy?" the boy asked, tucking his chin in as he pushed his head against the high pile of soft pillows, his dark hair falling perfectly into his eyes.

The man approached him and saw and wiped the ejaculate from his groin and pubic hair with the tip of the towel.

The young man stretched his arms and legs and squirmed in the sheets. Drops of cum continued to accumulate at the head of his penis.

"Ooooohhh, I think I got your sheets all sticky, Jimmy. Is that a problem, that I got your sheets all sticky?" He inserted a finger into his mouth and pulled it out with a popping sound, slapping his hard stomach with his right hand and said, "Ahhhhhh, Jimmy, I feel so good."

Suddenly, he emitted a long, loud fart and laughed.

"Oh, Jimmy, your poor sheets!"

And the boy threw the top sheet up and off his body, so that it fluttered down again, covering the whole of him, from head to feet.

As the cloth settled, Frame studied the shape of him as he rattled with laughter, his form a bas-relief map of desire. The wide shoulders, the carved chest, the penis still nearly erect, the legs long and lean, the huge feet, hands and head.

His hands appeared again on the topside of the sheet and yanked it down over his mussed hair and his face, holding it tightly at the chin, like a frightened virgin.

He looked a Frame is if seeing him for the first time.

"Hey, Jimmy," he said, hitting the word with a low note in his otherwise high pitched voice. "What about you?"

Frame reached a hand up under his shirt and scratched his stomach and said nothing.

"Come here," said Chase.

Frame went to the bed again and sat. From under the sheet, he could feel the curve of the boy's body as it smoothed around him.

"Do you want me to help you?" the youth asked.

And his hand moved close to the erection that still stood out from between Frame's legs. The young man hesitated and then, with just the light touch of the tips of his fingers he stroked the head of the older man's penis.

Frame shuddered and closed his eyes.

"Does that feel good, Jimmy?"

It did. His touch, this touch, this perfect, longed-for contact with the object of his love and lust rendered Jameson Frame quite speechless.

He nodded.

"What else do you want me to do, Jimmy?" Chase asked in a husky whisper.

Frame opened his eyes to the rasp of the voice, hoping to see on his face a sign of desire. But the youth had closed his eyes and his face was a perfect mask of immaculate disinterest, his calm symmetrical features showing nothing.

Frame said to Chase, "I think I will take a shower," and went into the bathroom to leave the youth to do as he liked.

Under cover of the hot steam, Frame pleasured himself, recalling all that he had seen through the lens of his camera and how Chase had played with him through it, revealing that which he wanted to reveal: the look on his face as the moment came in which he knew he could not hold back any longer, the arch of his back, the curl of his toes, the grunt, and the moan that accompanied his orgasm. The moment in which his beautiful face seemed ugly, when his heavy brow pushed down into his face and a guttural "Uh, uh, uuuhhhh," caught in his throat. He'd loved how Chase's face and neck turned quite red and the roughness with which he clutched his own organ. He loved the sweat on him, the scent of it and of his cum filling the room. He loved that he and he alone could smell it, could feel the stickiness of it as he wiped him gently with the towel.

He loved the fact that he found it all quite beautiful as it unfolded, as the boy gave himself unstintingly to the camera. His beauty made the act one of supreme beauty. His slow build to an explosive orgasm captured for all time like an object caught in amber. This brief moment caught forever, when a boy at the peak of his youth and beauty shared the pleasures of his body in innocence and simplicity.

They had, it seemed, made art.

When Frame came out of the bathroom, his bathrobe on and tied, he found Chase at the desk in the sitting room, with the camera again attached to the laptop, playing with the edits. He still was nude except for the towel that he had draped now around his shoulders. He seemed to be totally unconcerned about his nudity.

"Come and see this, Jimmy," he said with some excitement. "I think you're gonna like it."

Looking over his shoulder, he watched the boy juggle images on the screen, with multiple windows showing multiple takes. As he watched a brief moment of what may well have been, the finished product appeared from a series of quick cuts and quick edits.

The boy clicked on a switch. On the screen, his face disappeared in slow motion under the curtain of water.

He froze the motion on the screen and asked, simply, "Huh?" His eyes were bright.

Frame went down on his haunches and looked more closely at the screen as the cycle of images repeated. He looked up into the boy's face. "How did you learn to do this," he asked.

"High school," the boy mumbled, his concentration focused on the screen in front of him, an image of him writhing in the shower. Chase turned and spoke. "Jimmy, why don't you get some sleep? I want to work on this and try and get it done as soon as possible."

With a nod, Frame got up and walked into the bedroom, closed the door and got into his empty bed.

He'd turned off the lights as he went, and so laid there in darkness, save for the light that spilled in from under the door. He felt at once a pull to that light, to where he might sit and lay his head on the boy's bare thigh while Chase clattered away at the keyboard and swore under his breath, and a pull as well to envelop himself in the scent that clung to the sheets around him and sleep.

In the end that was enough, to lie where Chase had lain not long before, to smell him, to perhaps feel a little of the heat of him, fading now, but his presence still so strong, as if he had slept in the same spot in this bed for twenty years, had left a deep impression of his body, sick, well, happy, sad, aging, even sagging, but beautiful, eternally beautiful, always nude and sexual, lying here in the spot where Frame now lay, his own robe discarded as he walked, his body nude where the youth had been nude.

And Jameson Frame pulled the sheets around himself and slept.

When next he opened his eyes, there was soft sunlight in the room. He awakened to the sensation of his own erection pressing against the sheets, tenting them. He folded his arms behind his head and grinned.

He realized then that he had been awakened by the sound of a tapping at the bedroom door. He heard a voice from the other side calling, "Jimmy? Jimmy?"

"Uh huh," he answered, sleep still in his voice.

The door opened and Chase walked in the room, still naked, holding a large tray laden with food. He brought the tray over to the bed and set it down and seated himself.

"What's this?" Frame asked, rubbing his eyes.

"I ordered stuff from room service for us. Okay to do that?"

"Yes, okay to do that, but you didn't answer the door like that, did you?"

"Nah," Chase laughed. "I put the towel back on."

He poured a cup of strong coffee for Frame, who sat up in bed to receive it. Chase then removed the covers from various plates to show him eggs, bacon, toast, and sliced fruit. Frame shook his head to each of them.

"Just have some coffee," he said. "It's more than enough."

"There's juice, too, in the other room."

"Ah," said the older man.

Chase took hold of Frame's ankles then and pushed them up to force him to bend his knees. The youth then rested himself in the crook of Frame's legs and sighed. Feeling the press of the man's erection, the boy snickered but did not move. Instead, he wriggled his shoulders, pressing himself against it.

"Dude, that video is fucking awesome," he said. "The Chasers are going to go out of their fucking minds."

"Have you finished?" asked Frame.

"No, I got a ways to go yet, but, man!"

"Is it art?" asked Frame, putting down his cup.

"It's art, Jimmy," said the boy, turning his attention to the tray. "You sure you don't want any?"

"Me? No. You eat."

And he did. Sitting with his knees bent and his ankles crossed at the bottom of the bed, Chase ate the eggs, the bacon, the toast, even the fruit with great relish. He ate until there was nothing left to eat. Ate until he laid the tray on the floor and stretched himself out across the bed.

Frame shifted himself so that he, too, lay across the bed, his body on his right side, close to where Chase lay on his back. His torso still lay under the sheets, his legs and arms free of encumbrance.

As Frame worked his courage up to the point of laying the flat of his hand across the lower part of Chase's abdomen, just above the pubic patch, eyeing his target zone with a ferocity that he feared might burn the boy's skin, Chase said, "So here's the thing, Jimmy, I've got a really good rhythm going. So I thought you might want to go and see the ladies while I keep on working and then we could meet back here later. Okay?"

"Are they here?" asked Frame.

Chase motioned with his head. Frame sat up on the mattress and looked out at the beach. Below, he could see two beefy men setting up what could only be the sukkah.

"When the guys start setting that up, they're sure to arrive soon," said the youth. "And I can only imagine how our Elsa's been missing you. 'Oh, Jameson,' she'll say," said Chase with his voice pitched high and coated in a strange gypsy accent. "I haff been so vorried about you." And he opened his eyes wide and drove them into the man's face.

"And then she'll say," said the boy, dragging his arm down on the floor, reaching something, "'You muss haff a stawverry,'" he said, lifting the fruit plate up at Frame.

"Must be driving the old girls crazy, dude, not knowing where you are."

"Ummm . . ." said Frame, unsure.

"Just give me two hours, Jimmy. Three. Three hours, Jimmy. I just want to get this done and then we can take my car and go out somewhere." He thought a moment and brightened. "I can take you back to that doctor who butchered you yesterday and make him do something about it. And about that little belly of yours."

His attention drawn to the slight paunch around his waist, Frame recoiled and sat up, his legs over the side of the bed. He reached over and picked up from the bedside table the card that Kyle had given him. He dialed the number and gave his name and was told that he could come in at one that afternoon and that both the nodules and his belly could be tended to. He was told that in the meantime he should not eat.

"It's a good thing I didn't have any of that breakfast," he told Chase as he hung up the phone. "We're to be there at one."

"Okay, Jimmy," said Chase, who quite suddenly pushed his face close into Frame's and quite deliberately kissed him hard and deeply. The youth held the man firmly by the shoulders and plunged his tongue deeply into Frame's mouth, penetrating deeply. They stayed like this, lips gently sliding over one another. Frame then tried to lift his arms to embrace the boy, to pull him tight, to own him, but Chase held him firm. Their chests touched, their hearts pounded into each other's ribs. Their breathing slammed them haphazardly together. Their pricks rose up hard and Chase swung his to knock against the man and then slid himself against the man's soft stomach.

Frame pushed in closer, hungry for the boy. Chase pulled his mouth away and then bit Frame lightly on his bottom lip. He surrounded his mouth with the softest of kisses, inhaling the breath from the older man's lungs as he did so. Frame, rendered breathless, slumped in the boy's grip. And the boy kissed him once more and then let go.

"Thanks, Jimmy," he said and got up off the bed, his cock swinging in front of him.

From the other room, Frame could hear the sound of the video, the sound of his own voice saying, "Now look at me, Chase, look directly at me," with the sound of the shower running in the background.

Frame got out of bed and dressed slowly, reluctantly, from his trove of new clothes. He chose a baggy long swimsuit and a matching hooded jacket from his endless wardrobe. He slipped on flip-flops that had been beautifully made from soft leather and gathered up his exquisite watch, which he clipped on his wrist and put his keycard in his pocket.

He walked quietly into the other room, and instantly smelled the aroma of Chase's drug. The joint hung from his lips as he stared intently at the computer screen.

Frame walked over and put his arms around the boy and whispered in his ear, "Just be careful with that stuff, okay?"

Chase absent-mindedly shrugged off the embrace, saying, "Nice watch, Jimmy."

The man kissed the boy on the top of his head. The youth registered no response, but, as the man walked toward the door said simply,

"See you later, Jimmy."

And, as instructed, the man went out the door.

TWENTY-TWO

~~~

As he crossed the wide doorway of the sukkah, Jameson Frame saw that Elsa was seated alone, her legs tucked under her. A stronger wind than usual pressed against the batik walls, first from one side then from the other. The sea to the front was disquieted, iron colored.

Not feeling or hearing his presence, Elsa sat looking at a large round brass tray that sat upon a low Moroccan table in front of her. On it was a vast array of fruits, vegetables, dips, oils, honey and flowers.

She looked up, momentarily startled by Frame's presence. He spoke to her, but she could not hear, over the sound of the wind and the sea and whoops of the surfers riding the high chortles of waves. Elsa waved him into the relative quiet of her room. She slid over to allow him to join her behind her table, as they both watched the rough plumage of the sea. "The Pacific gives lie to its name today," said Elsa, who then returned her attention to the platter in front of her.

"Look, Jameson," she said, clapping her hands with delight. "It is a Garden of Earthy Delights!" She lifted a large, lush strawberry with the fingers of her left hand and brought her right hand, cupped under it, guiding both slowly toward the target of Frame's lips. Seeing it, he thought somehow of a priest offering communion.

"Here," said Elsa. "Take it. Delicious."

He took the sweet berry in his mouth, admired the red pulp with his tongue and swallowed it, smiling.

"It is so good to see you, Jameson!" She exclaimed, and yet, in her exclamation of joy there was a tone of reproach as well. "I was getting worried about you."

"As you can see," he said, "I am quite well, and in your continuing debt in terms of my wardrobe."

"It's good to see you," he added after a pause, before asking, "Where's Vera? Is she unwell?"

"Oh, no. She is perfectly well. She had some business to discuss with our lawyer and thought that I would prefer the ocean's company to his." She issued a breathy laugh. "You see how well she knows me. And how sweetly our friends from the gym treat me—to bring me such a feast and leave it as a surprise!"

A reeling screech overhead brought Frame to his knees as he peered over the top of the sukkah. Gulls played overhead, pressing hard against the wild wind and then allowing themselves to be buffeted freely by it in the vastness of the wide mauve sky.

When he drew himself back into the room, Elsa was digging in her woven bag.

"Vera sent something for you. She told me that I should meet you today. She is usually right about such things, of course. And I should be more accustomed to that fact after all these years and had her offering at the ready—Ah, here it is!"

She placed one hand over the other, the other under, the thing sandwiched in between and she dawdled with it, keeping it low and out of eyesight, as if blessing it or bidding it adieu and finally she placed it in his warm dry upraised palm.

It weighed nothing. The thing was wrapped in a piece of silk scarf the color of the sea on a sunny day. He untied the simple knot and the silk melted away, showing the card, The Hanged Man. As placed in his palm, it sat facing him, inverted against his body.

As he recognized the gift, Elsa busied herself with the contents of her platter, dipping some pineapple into chocolate and swallowing it down.

Frame's eyes narrowed. How he wanted to tear the card again and again, and then let the wind carry the bits of it off to sea.

Instead, he placed it in the pocket of his jacket, so that The Hanging Man, inverted, stood facing his heart.

"You must thank Vera for me for her loving gift," he said simply. He handed her the piece of blue silk, which she wound, in turn, around her hair and wrapped finally around her neck, knotting it against the wind that licked up and into the tent. She gathered a handful of flowers, kissed them, tossed them into the breeze, and looked at him and smiled.

Frame rested himself against the thick soft pillow and he faced Elsa with his profile. As the day was dark, he took off his sunglasses and set them on the table.

Looking over at him, Elsa brought her fingers up to her lips in horror. She gasped. "Jameson," she said, "your eyes. Surely this is not some response . . ."

"I'm afraid it is," he said.

"It looks as if it were frightfully painful."

"Yes, they are rather painful." He turned his head from side to side to show her the angry wens.

"Oh, Jameson."

"They say it happens sometimes. Some sort of reaction to the injections. I am told that it is nothing dangerous and that it will fade in time."

"Oooooohhhhhhhh," she made the sound of a wounded animal as he spoke. "You must let me help you," she said. "I could call and make an appointment for you. Surely Dr. Magellan . . ."

"I've already taken care of it. I have an appointment this afternoon."

"I would be happy to go with you in the town car if you like."

Frame smiled at her. "Actually there is no need, Elsa," he said, the warmth that the news he was about to share gave him a literal twinge of joy. "Chase is going to take me in his car."

Elsa frowned. She sat very still for a long time, holding her knees together in front of her with her arms, her hands hiding her ruby-painted toenails. Her chin rested lightly against her knees.

A group of children ran past their tent, screaming, they turned to look inside as they ran past. One child twisted his face at Frame, sticking out his tongue and shouting, "Faggot!" as he went hurtling past.

Long behind the children, an overweight woman came running. She shouted at them, "Stay out of the ocean, damn it," as she went running past, clutching a large woven bag, in the top of which sat a large plastic bottle of water, a paperback book and a tube of suntan lotion that bobbled in time with her breasts.

To the front and side of the opening, Frame could see a man walking slowly down by the lip of the ocean, sweeping a metal detector in front of him. He concentrated on the man and his steady motion—a step forward and a sweep to the right and one to the left before the next step—during their awkward silence.

Elsa sighed, rather more loudly than she usually did, perhaps to be heard over the sounds of the rough winds and water.

"Jameson," she said, "I feel I must warn you."

He put up his hand rather forcefully, to silence her.

She covered part of his large hand with her much smaller one. He was reminded in that instant of an infant's hand and how insistently they can use their tiny fingers. She looked at him rather intently.

"The simple truth, Jameson," she began, as if stating the first sentence of a long, long story, "is that he is not who he appears to be." She paused meaningfully and then nodded her head toward him once, twice.

"We love him quite dearly, Vera and I and Bobo and Kiki and all the rest of us who live here with him. We loved him from when we first saw him skateboarding by what was it, weeks or months perhaps, more than a year ago. One forgets time here, and tends to remember only occurrences— the new face, some shocking turn of events, or the weather on a day like this. So odd. Sometimes, Vera and I will refer to something by saying, remember that it happened on the day when the water was like it was being heated in a giant tea kettle? We mark our lives by this.

"So it was when one of us first noticed our Chase on his skateboard, such a beautiful boy. How he flew past and back again and past again with feats of daring do. And how he would fall and bloody himself but if someone should offer to help him he'd wave them away and do the stunt again and again until he mastered it. Riding on the ridges of things, on benches, using the street as a ramp. Anything. He would always have names for these things as well, names the rest of us could not understand. But colorful, so colorful. And so beautiful.

"By the time he came to a rest, there were always scabs and bruises and lumps. The only one from whom he would accept help was Mikey, his beloved Mikey, always by his side, always in the shadows, just out of reach. And yet, he was the only one who could ever touch our Chase." She laughed lightly.

"Chase. I can't remember now if that was the name he called himself, or a name that someone gave him. It seemed to suit him. In motion, always in motion. Like a puppy that runs and stops and waits to be chased. Who grows so sad if no one chases him . . ."

"Will Mikey be going with you to the doctor's office this afternoon?" she asked.

"No, I don't think so," said Frame, who had not given the brother a thought.

"Ah," said Elsa, nodding. And then, almost under her breath, she added, "Dear dear dear . . ."

"You must understand, Jameson, that this place is one of those places. Vera says that here, right here under the place on which we build our sukkah, there is a vortex, a small spot on which the energies of many dimensions intertwine and dance. That is also why we have our drum circles here, right here, to allow ourselves to partake of the universe's fizz. Think of how you yourself felt here only a little time ago, how light-headed the dance made you.

"This energy calls to people, Jameson, it called to you. Although you felt your decision a whim, it called you. As it calls so many others, in moments of discontent or discord or confusion.

"That's why so many who pass through here are so very young, dear Jameson, because they seek some sense of explanation of the nature of things, these myriad realities. Most seek some definition of self. And so you find so many, young and old"—did she look meaningfully at Jameson Frame as she said this?—"coming here for self discovery."

She unwrapped the silk scarf from her head. It was caught in a sudden updraft as she did so. The wind whipped the scarf into its full length and snapped it out of her hand and up, up into the sky out of sight. Elsa looked startled and then laughed. She bent her head out of the sukkah, in order to spot the scarf but could not. Her hair flew up about her face giving it a prickly effect, her short gray hair like the burr of a spent dandelion.

"We see so many boys like Chase here, Jameson. Almost daily, they get off buses or trains or whatever the young people use besides the skateboard. They come to the beach, often blending in with the rest of the visitors. And yet, something in their eyes says that they, unlike the others, have no home or hotel to go back to. That this place, this damp beach, a portal to so many dimensions, is their new home.

"So it was with dear Chase and with his beloved Mikey. And so they clung to each other, sleeping with asses touching like dogs so that none could get close without awakening them. Wary, always wary, in the way young puppies always are.

"You see, back home—and I have been told that home for Chase is somewhere far from here, somewhere carved by glaciers—the boy had been noticed for his beauty and had been taken to a photographer who got him work in catalogs and local television at quite a young age and then, still when he was very young, had introduced the boy to what he called art photography. He taught the boy a bit about how to use his eyes when looking into a camera and how best to arrange his genitalia to thickest effect. And he taught the boy to be quite comfortable conveying a message of sexuality to the camera.

"One photographer lent him to another, the 'artists' being rather like foster fathers all seeking payment of one sort or another for every lesson they had to offer.

"Finally, one photographer gave him to another who lived in Los Angeles, and the boy came willingly here, and worked, actually worked for a while, making good money, his face and body on billboards in some lovely underwear.

"Things must have seemed quite promising to him just then, living in that photographer's home, swimming in his pool, sleeping in his bed. But what the boy did not know was that other boys just like him were arriving by the truckload, skate-load, or whatever, and that he, by the time he had reached his peak on the billboards, was already passé.

"Can you think of it, Jameson, to be, what, eighteen perhaps, or even less—could it have been only sixteen, fifteen—and to be already passé? To be born with that face, to sculpt that body, to grow to perfection and yet, and yet to be considered rather dull and tired once you have been seen and touched and used?

"They say that he is rather heavily into drugs, Jameson. That he picked up the habit at that photographer's house, where all things were on offer. They say that, if it were not for the tattoos and the scraps and scabs, the needle marks would show more. And they say that it was his own treachery that got the photographer's door slammed in his face and started his slow spiral downward until he and his 'brother' came to be sleeping here on the beach, ass to ass."

She sighed, as if finished.

"Do you wish to know more?"

Frame shook his head. And yet she continued.

"Then high time you began to ask yourself what you already know. Ask yourself if you have ever seen two 'brothers' who seem so little alike. Ask yourself if you ever feel at rest with the boy or if you, like all the rest, are chasing, always chasing. Ask yourself if you ever for a moment have felt as if he saw you for you, the lovely middle-aged man that you are, or only saw another photographer with his door open to him, waiting to shoot him, to open him up with his camera, to make 'art'"—she said the word bitterly, ruefully—"with him until someone shuts the door. Ask yourself if there is parity here, or honesty here, or even real possibility here—"

Frame arose.

Without a word, he left the tent, stepped back into the cold and damp wind that was in no way warmed by the distant feckless sun. He stuffed his sunglasses into the breast pocket, bending the Tarot card, and strode, clearing the ropes binding the tent frame into the stakes driven deep deep into the sand, and walking to the door of the Hotel des Bains.

He had only taken two or three steps before he heard the catastrophic sound. The clamor of the overturning of the low Moroccan table and the large brass tray, which scattered the feast garden of earthly delights to the four winds. And worse, something worse, he heard also something like a shriek, more guttural than the calling of the gulls, as he steadily walked away.

TWENTY-THREE

∽

When Jameson Frame let himself into his suite at the Hotel des Bains, he was struck by the silence of the place. There was no sign of the boy, only his detritus. And only his scent—the funk of him and of his drugs, intermixed—that had permeated the rooms.

He saw the door to the bedroom slightly ajar and pushed it, carefully, so that it revealed the sole of Chase's foot at the bottom of the bed. Seeing it, and hearing the slow, steady sound of his sleep-soaked breathing, he closed the door with caution.

It was then, as his head was turning away, that he saw the note stuck against the computer keyboard.

On it, in a childish scrawl that mixed cursive with block print, Chase had first written a short commentary on how to work the machine and then, simply, noted the existence of a video that had been placed at the center of the screen.

At the bottom of the note were two simple words: "Play it," and a line drawing of a skateboard with a skull illustrating the bottom of the page.

Frame lifted the chair and pulled it out silently. He seated himself, flipped the computer on and leaned back, waiting for the whirling wheel to give way to the colored screen.

When the thing was fully alive, he saw, in the center of the screen, as promised, a smaller video screen embedded. He pressed "play" and immediately muted the thing against the noise that issued full volume. On the screen, the word "Chase" appeared and faded, with the words: "I Want To Share My Whole Life With You" appearing and then fading away. Finally the single word "Wet" appeared and the image of Chase's ridged stomach, with streams of water playing down his muscles and dragging his body hair downward. His face appeared, full frame, with a look mixing what seemed vaguely like stupor with a full flowering of lust. His eyes were nearly closed, his brows had beads of water clinging to them, and then rolling away, slicking down his face. He bit his lower lip and the tip of his tongue thrust through his lips and slicked them. His liquid lips shaped themselves slowly, meaningfully into the slightest of smiles.

From there, the three minutes and nine seconds of the video unrolled, with the images that they together had filmed in his bathroom. There was the boy, whose odor perfumed the place, the boy who slept now in his bed, displayed in full erotic fantasy in his own upscale hotel suite.

Frame found the volume control and was able to unmute it and listen as well as watch. In his editing, the youth had mixed his audio skillfully enough, catching at times the sound of a sign issuing from his own lips, or the whisper of his breathing, or, at the end, when he brought the towel up over his ass and back, arching it into the air like batwings before allowing it to fall back down on the top of his wet hair, which he scrubbed dry, with a bark-like laugh, which melted into a simmering titter as the video image faded to a solid red background and the words again: *I Want To Share My Whole Life With You,* followed by a copyright sign and the date before the final fade to black.

A little "humph," slipped out from Frame's lips as he leaned back in the desk chair. In life, Chase was the most beautiful man that Frame had ever seen. And yet.

And yet, on video, he was something more.

Frame sat, pondering the nature of it, the presence that the boy had in front of the camera—the camera in his hands. Had the lens somehow made what was already perfect even more so? Or had it perhaps captured the image of the boy that Frame carried inside of himself and somehow allowed that image, that idea of the ideal, to be shared?

Frame touched the screen lightly with the tips of the fingers of his right hand. Touched the image of Chase's face where it had been frozen by Frame, just at the point where the hint of the smile appeared—that hint of a smile being something that he had seen often enough already to associate it with the words, "Oh, Jimmy," and with the notion that he was himself quite hopeless.

In that moment, his face reddened with a mixture of embarrassment and desire. He felt as if it were he who were nude for the world to see and not Chase, as it was, he saw now, his own depraved desire for the boy that was the subject of the shoot, no matter its title.

He arose from the desk and saw, nearby, the pile of clothing that Chase had left in the room, along with the wrappers of his food, his opened backpack and the plastic sandwich bag of drugs that lay unzipped on the coffee table.

Frame reached down and picked up the pile of clothes. By instinct, he pulled them up to his face and inhaled deeply, closing his eyes. He squeezed the clothes as tightly to him as he could. Would have rubbed them up against him in another moment, but he heard, coming from the other room, a single sigh.

He opened the bedroom door. Opened it wide.

And saw the full length of the boy, the entirety of his body, naked, wrapped only in the softness of the hotel's perfect sheet.

And Chase awoke, his head still plunged downward in the pillows he had nested around him. He pushed himself up with his right arm, and Frame saw the mark of his billowing tattoo.

Chase looked up at him, the top of his head still resting in feathers. He grinned, wide, his teeth the perfect white puppy teeth.

"Morning, Jimmy," he said and then coughed his smoker's cough.

"Time to get dressed," said Jameson Frame. "We've got to go now."

While Chase drove erratically through the city streets, Frame took out his wallet and fanned in front of him the business cards that he had so far gathered. He plucked one away from the others and showed it to Chase.

"Do you know where this is?" he asked the boy.

"Yeah," he answered.

"I want to stop there first, okay?"

And Chase nodded his head and stepped on the gas and his Ford Falcon sped along.

Soon, they were at the same shop that Elsa had introduced him to. He found that clerk who had assisted him, handed him his credit card and, indicating Chase, said, "Get him anything he wants."

The boy's eyes sparkled. He mouthed the word "Jimmy."

"Dude," he mouthed back, winking.

"Oh, and I want him to have a blue suit. Single breasted. We've got no time to have it tailored, so it will have to be off the rack. Plus shoes, belt, a white dress shirt, and a tie. I'll pick out the tie. Just bring me some to choose from."

And turning Chase over to the clerk, Frame seated himself on the comfortable couch near the back of the store and stared out the window.

Sitting there, he found that he felt old, paternal. And that his temples pounded as if the skin of his forehead had been stretched over a series of little spikes. His left leg continued to throb, making each step a new source of discomfort. So he sat; and he crossed his left leg up over the right in order to loosen the fabric of his pants away from his leg.

By the time they were finished, the trunk of the Falcon was crammed with packages. Chase had watched the boxing of his new wardrobe with gleaming eyes. Those eyes were now covered as he drove them to Dr. Magellan's office with oversized sunglasses with wide tortoise-shell frames. As he drove, he occasionally looked over at Frame in order to dazzle him with a smile. As he parked near the office, his hand dropped to Frame's thigh and squeezed.

As he emerged from the wreck of his still-rattling car in one of his new outfits, a light jacket, shirt, slacks and shoes that covered his tattoos, the young man looked fit, handsome and wealthy.

Standing on the sidewalk in front of the Cotswald cottage, Frame suddenly felt a sense of panic. He took Chase by the arm and asked if he had anything that could help him with the fear and pain he was about to experience. The boy grinned, quietly said, "Dude" and got his Ziploc bag out of his backpack in the trunk of the car.

They entered Dr. Magellan's office, much to the abrupt attention of his female staff. Frame found himself relegated to the couch after his presence was acknowledged. Sitting there, he fought the temptation to allow his eyes to roll back in his head, as the pill the boy had given him began to take effect. He listened to the gentle sounds of conversation and to the music that was piped into the room. A shaft of sunlight fell across his lap from the window nearby, warming him. And he felt the deep, twitchy desire for sleep.

He was awakened some time later and opened his eyes to see Kyle looming over him and calling him by name. He followed him into a room in the back, where the skin around his eyes was checked, first by Kyle and then again by Dr. Magellan, both of whom agreed that everything was coming along nicely and that Frame, when he returned to Manhattan, should visit his doctor there in order to continue his treatment.

"Now," said Dr. Magellan, about that other matter.

Frame was instructed to remove his shirt and he stood in front of the doctor and his assistant. They looked at him a good time, sometimes pointing to specific parts of his body, other times drawing circles on him with a purple felt-tipped marker.

"Jameson," said Magellan at last, turning his patient so that he could see all of Frame's body in the reflection of the mirror in front of them.

"You are an ideal candidate for what we call tumescent liposuction. This means that the entire procedure can be done with local anesthetic and can be done here in the office today."

He pointed to the area of Frame's stomach. "As you can see, this is the major area of importance. From here, we can remove approximately two to three pounds of excess fat. From the sides, here and here," he said, indicating Frame's slight love handles, "we can remove another pound."

"Now, finally, from here," he said, indicating the underside of Frame's chin, "we can remove a little more to stop the formation of the wattle and to tighten your jawline."

"Wattle?" Frame asked.

"Now, tumescent liposuction has been in existence since the late 1980s and is therefore a tried and true method of working. We introduce into your system a high but very diluted dose of lidocaine to act as the local anesthetic and use epinephrine to constrict your capillaries. This helps us to trap the fat that is to be removed and also serves to stop bleeding.

"We then punch a series of very small holes into your skin. These holes are called 'adits' and are a single millimeter long. Small enough that they require no stitches to close the wounds and also small enough that they heal very quickly.

"We remove the excess fat, giving you a trimmer, more youthful appearance. You may feel a slight nausea afterward, and your skin may be a bit tender from the places where the needles entered and the adits are healing, but, by and large, you will be able to return to your regular activities immediately with only the slightest discomfort."

He looked at Frame, blinking.

"Yes," said Frame, "I would like to carry on with the procedure today."

"Very good," said Dr. Magellan, who nodded at Frame and then at Kyle and then left the room.

"The fact that we don't need stitches means that there is very little swelling, Jameson, which is a good thing," said Kyle conspiratorially. "Stitches hold in fluids, which means that swelling is bigger and lasts longer, while the body reabsorbs the fluids. This way, you may experience a little drainage from the adits, a little fluid loss and the fluid may have a rosy color from the blood in it, but it means that you will be well and looking trim and fresher much sooner."

As he talked, he helped Frame out of his clothing, which he hung neatly in a locker in the rear of the room, and into a hospital gown.

As he finished, the door opened and two young attendants, each vibrant in her smooth beauty, took Frame down to a room in the back. Here they rested him on a hospital bed, raised the head of it a bit for his comfort and stepped back, smiling but silent, until Dr. Magellan and Kyle reentered the room, each dressed in a surgical gown.

"Why don't you just sleep now?" Kyle asked, lidocaine in hand.

And Frame did as he was told.

When he came to—moments, minutes, hours later—he felt immediately an odd pestering of his skin. Looking down at his uncovered stomach, he could see nothing, no redness, no swelling, but felt as if small insects were inside his skin, biting it, chewing on him from within.

One of the beauties stepped into his sight range and called Kyle by name.

He stepped over and told Frame that he had come through the procedure perfectly and that he now had the smooth stomach of a twenty-year-old. That he should eat simple things for the next day or two, as the very diluted drugs would remain in his system for up to thirty-six hours, which would leave him feeling some degree of analgesia for that period of time. And that this analgesia would keep him from feeling any sense of discomfort while the adits healed as well.

Lying there and taking stock, Frame could feel no pain in any part of his body. He felt himself relax into the bed as he had not been able to do since experiencing the tattoo needle.

When he dressed and returned to the waiting room, he found Chase waiting for him, a white paper bag on his lap.

"What's in there?" he asked.

"Some stuff," Chase answered.

Frame walked over to the desk, signed all documents thrust in front of him and again gave over his credit card to pay the bill, that, he noticed, contained charges for several different kinds of unguents and creams.

They made one more stop on the way back to the hotel. One stop that Frame insisted upon, even when told it was not necessary. One stop that Frame felt was entirely necessary, perhaps because of his anesthetized state.

Once Bucky got over the sight of Chase in long pants and a dress shirt and shoes, and once he had asked for the tenth time, "What's up with you?" he shoved up Frame's pant leg and looked at his work, with a muttered, "Oh, yeah," indicating the moment at which he remembered this old man, who wept and clung to his assistant's hand.

"Alice ain't here today," Bucky said, shrugging.

Frame said, "Now, this is what I want," and described the finished tattoo, the original Roman V with the letter spelled out in Morse Code— dot dot dot dash—underneath.

"And all surrounded by a perfect red circle," said Frame. "The kind of chunky red circle that surrounds the icon for a brand," he said, sketching the circle with his fingertip on the skin around his tattoo.

For the finished image would be a brand of sorts.

"Think World War II. 'V for victory,'" concluded Frame.

"Oh, yeah?" asked Bucky, as, head downward, he prepared the needles and ink. "Before my time, man."

Chase went and sat at the front of the store, on a long, low sofa, and looked through books of tattoos and arose to open the door for Frame when he prepared to leave.

Bucky chortled at the sight of it. Chase glared back at him over the top of Frame's left shoulder.

Thanks in part to his lidocaine haze, Frame kept his tears inside his eyes and put his full weight on his left foot, limping only very slightly as they walked to the car, a small container of Bactine forgotten on the counter.

TWENTY-FOUR

༜

Moving quite languorously, Chase dropped the white paper bag on the couch, gathered up his zip bag from his backpack and walked into the bedroom. Frame carried with him, slung over his arm, the boy's new blue suit. He set it and the bag containing the rest of the outfit carefully on the couch and followed the boy.

Chase sat on the bed with his legs spread wide and lit another joint, his eyes half closed.

"Have I showed you this, Jimmy?" he asked and then inhaled deeply, leaving his jaw slack. He then allowed the smoke to blossom from his mouth and inhaled it again through his nostrils, before releasing it all and allowing the cloud of vapor to swirl around his head. He tipped his head sideways at Frame. "That's called a 'French Inhale,' Jimmy. You want to try it?"

Frame took the joint from his hand and sucked on it hard, but simply let the smoke billow where it would. Then he walked into the bathroom and turned the spigot on in the deep, jetted bath, full force, feeling the complaints of the adits as he did so.

He walked back into the bedroom, slipping the joint back in the youth's waiting mouth and, with steady, confident hands, unbuttoned the top button of Chase's shirt. He had expected, should this moment come, with the fabric coating the youth's skin actually in reach, that his hands would shake, his mouth would go dry, and yet, he felt more steady in this moment than he had in any moment since his arrival in Venice.

Chase allowed his head to wallow a bit, relaxed, and watched Frame with hooded eyes. A second button, a third. And then Frame pulled the shirt from his pants, took it from the boy and laid it gently on the bed.

He offered Chase his hand and helped him to arise. They walked, hands clasped, into the bathroom.

"Hey, Jimmy," said Chase, "thanks, Jimmy," he continued and, all in a moment attempted to gather the older man in his arms and kiss him.

This Frame resisted. He brought Chase to the edge of the bath.

"Not now," he said, slipping the belt from around the boy's waist. "Now I want to do this."

And he undressed the boy and helped him into the deep, hot tub. The youth allowed the man to maneuver him and then to wash him.

Frame got his own shaving kit and laid out his tools across the tiled floor in easy reach. He was on his knees then, next to the tub, his right arm under the boy's neck, coddling him, the sleeve of his shirt already soaked, the front of it stained with splashes of water and light ruby-red sites of discharge. He felt the pain with every movement, pain now present in every part of his body. And he felt the heat begin to accumulate in his chest and in his head.

He slid his hand from behind the boy's head, replacing it with a rolled towel. The boy adjusted his posture, his head thrown back, his legs covered in the deep water.

Frame drew his hand across the boy's neck and touched his lips. The boy snickered. He then drew his hand down, through the scrape of the boy's beard to the hair of his chest and across to each nipple. He rubbed his palm against the concrete of his abdomen, the ridges carved through years of strategy and work. He turned his hand so that the back of his fingers teased against the trail of hair that began at his navel and followed it below the water, looking up as he did so, seeing nothing but those same hooded eyes.

He took the boy's cock in his hand and stroked it, felt it harden within his grasp. He ran his thumb across the tip of it, feeling the sponge of it, pulling more and harder, with insistent rhythm. When the organ was completely erect, he let it go and played instead with the boy's balls, moving them in his hand and holding them tight. His hand moved then behind them, finding the crack of the boy's ass, penetrating it with a single finger.

And the boy moaned.

He took his hand away then and, noticing the gathering of red on his own chest, leaned away enough to remove his own shirt. Looking down, he saw the angry swelling of his belly and the traces of red in the hair on his chest. Reaching a thick towel, he placed it between the tub and himself to absorb the discharges and leaned in again to the boy. He gathered up a thick washcloth and the goat-milk soap and scrubbed the boy, beginning with his feet.

He scanned the boy's skin, bit by bit, segment by segment, searched him with his hands, touching every part, intruding everywhere. He was alert with every sense, seeking out needle trails, wounds, bruises, he knew not what, really. He felt inadequate for the job. And yet he touched him in adoration and the boy allowed him access.

He cleaned him. He scoured him. He dug the filth from the boy's toe-nails, and pumiced the rough patches on the soles of his feet. He cleaned the scratches, the scabs and the bruises that he attributed to the boy's skateboarding. Rubbed and scrubbed his skin at every point of his body.

When he had finished with his task, the boy's skin had attained a ruddy glow. He sat quite regally in his bath, enjoying the last moment in which, having scrubbed the boy's hair hard, with his own brand of shampoo, the man drenched him, pouring water straight down on his head and the boy laughed a hearty laugh, shaking his head and flinging the water wide across the whole of the room.

"That felt great," he said with a yawn.

He stood in front of the still-kneeling Frame, the water rushing from the lower part of his body, his still insistent prick inches from the man's face.

He stepped out of the tub and took the towel that Frame had leaned against and used it, quickly drying his body as he displayed it, first one leg up on the tub and then the other, and then draped it around his waist. As he walked to the sink, Frame could see the accumulation of red on the back of the towel.

Frame raised himself up and sat on the edge of the tub, watching, as the boy used his razor and soap to shave himself. As he leaned against the sink's edge, the towel fell away and the boy let it, showing Frame his rounded ass.

Seeing this, Frame wondered how it was that they had not, in their video session, recorded this act, exploring the sense of Eros thick in the room as the boy dragged the sharp razor over his thick beard, revealing the perfect boy's face beneath. Chase pursed his pink lips into a smooch that nearly touched the glass as he worked.

Finishing this, he turned to the older man and said quite simply, "Come here, Jimmy."

Frame joined him over by the sink.

As the older man stood there, the boy removed his clothing, tossing them into a heap in the corner by the trashcan. When removing Frame's left sock, he saw the finished tattoo and studied it, making a hissing noise at its mounded inflammation. He noticed the discharge against Frame's skin, the matted fur on his chest.

He took from Frame's shaving kit an electric razor and set it on the counter. He then stood next to the older man and roughly ran his hand through Frame's chest hair.

"I don't know how you stand it," he said with a sneer.

Taking the clippers in hand, he tore at the hair, rending it from Frame's tender skin. He sheered him in long strokes, as Frame stood, his head raised, his eyes wide.

Setting the clippers to a longer length, he trimmed the hair around the older man's cock and under his arms and, stepping back and looking closely, his head turning slightly from side to side, he issued a single "Ummpphh," and set the clippers down, much to Frame's relief.

Turning, the older man saw the results of the boy's efforts: a thousand little nicks and cuts across his now-smooth chest.

And to his horror, he caught the brightly lit reflection of his own face, taut with agony, swollen and mottled nearly beyond recognition, and yet smooth, and, somehow, eerily youthful.

His one blessing was that he somehow managed to convince the boy to wash him in the shower.

And so he stood there, warm water streaming, as the boy pressed his own body in behind him. "Did you enjoy polishing your trophy?" the boy asked him, whispering in his ear, making his skin tingle with lust and apprehension. He scrubbed him then, hard, with the loofah. His skin already afire now burned brightly within, chapped, aching, a tallow candle aflame.

The water off, the boy rubbed him hard with a soft towel. Finishing, Chase arose and they stood together in front of the mirrored sink wall, one pink, the other, fevered, one young, the other, old, oh, so old.

With the quality of their two suits, one blue and one black, encapsulating them, defining them, the two were treated with deference, as honored guests in the grand restaurant in the Hotel des Bains.

It occurred to Jameson Frame all at once both that this was the first time he had entered the restaurant, having taken most of his meals in his room, and that it seemed fitting that on the occasion of his first visit that the young man seated across from him should be with him, in that now he seemingly had moved into his suite as well.

Chase by candlelight, he noticed, was but a variant on all the other Chases, each a chiseled aspect of perfection. But here, in this place, in this moment—this was the Chase of preference, the one to be photographed and the photograph captured in a gilt frame.

As always, they relaxed together, with an apparent ease and simplicity of communication that belied the mystery of their bond. Chase looked slowly around the room, perhaps imagining its best camera angles, and returned his attention to Frame's face. Happy for the gentle glow of the candlelight, Frame smiled a wrinkle-free smile, showing teeth that he hoped were white enough.

"Any idea," he asked the boy, "what you might want to eat?"

Food was hefted in on silver trays and wine flowed freely, one bottle, then two. Red meat was eaten rare, and although Frame's system recoiled from the thought of it, he ate it, tore at it with his teeth, ripping and shredding and then swallowing without thinking.

Chewing, Frame felt the pulse of fluid discharging from the adits all on the underside of his chin and knew his shirt to be stained ruby-red where it had dampened his collar. Knew his temples had been Frankensteined with wens and welts and swellings and stings. Knew his concern for this to be vanishing more every moment with his ability to show emotion.

They ate the full list of aphrodisiacs, pointing at something new in the menu each time the waiter passed: asparagus in a fine rich hollandaise, oysters in a spicy stew, avocados stuffed with crabmeat, then figs and honey and strawberries. They drank a perfect cognac from thimble-sized glasses.

There was a ripeness in the moment, a beauty formed from the brief familiarity and the revelry of their intimacy. Frame, in spite of himself, relaxed against the plush softness of the place, ignoring the itch of his sheared skin and the wet stain that was spreading across his stomach and sides, allowing himself, all at once to be happy. Until happiness threatened, like the sea outside the door, to drown him in its embrace.

The boy reached his hand over and placed it on Frame's. He fingered at the thick gold of his exquisite watch and looked down at its face.

And then Chase said, "Jimmy, I have to go soon."

"Is it Mikey?" Frame asked.

"Huh? What?" the boy looked confused, and then, "No, it's not Mikey. He's fine."

"Do you want to go get him and bring him here? He can stay with us or I can get him his own room."

"No, Mikey's great. He's staying with some friends of ours. He doesn't like this part."

"Part?"

"Look, Jimmy, it's been great and I'll be back, but I have to go for a while. There's something that I have to get done, okay?"

"I don't like that you're always leaving," sighed Frame.

"And I don't like that you could leave at any time. I mean leave leave. With your suitcase. I don't like knocking on your locked door and not knowing if you're gone for good, Jimmy."

"Ah," said Frame, softly.

"Look," said the boy, "I'm not going anywhere and you're not going anywhere, okay?"

Sensing the boy's restlessness, Frame summoned the waiter and gave him his card. Outside, the wind blew rubble down the sidewalk in front of the window where they sat.

"It's such a bad night," said Frame. "Why not stay tonight and go tomorrow? What could you possibly have to do tonight?"

"Oh, fuck, Jimmy," said the youth, slamming the table and alarming the patrons in the shadowy room.

"I'll call you. Look, I will call you," he said, standing up. He placed his napkin carefully next to his plate and looked at it, as if hoping he had done the right thing. His face looked contorted as he rose, his forehead lined, his brow furrowed, a study in frustration, guilt, regret—an emotion Frame could not identify with any degree of surety.

"But I have to go now. Get some rest, Jimmy, you look awful."

And knowing as surely as Frame knew himself that he would never in such a place make a ruckus, the boy walked calmly out of the restaurant and turned toward the hotel's front door.

Frame sat waiting, then signed the chit for the meal and refused all offers of doggie bags and nightcaps. He stood, wobbly, aching and walked out of the place, willing his body to move calmly in a steady straight line.

Once past the sight of any of the diners, he ran as best he could for the front door, his own moist clothes cold against his fevered skin. He ran out into the cold, misty night, feeling the damp of the fog, the beginning of the precipitation. He walked a bit down the boardwalk to the place where he remembered leaving the boy's Falcon.

When he turned the corner he could see that the car was gone.

He turned and walked out of the cold, whipping wind and again into the warm embrace of the Hotel des Bains.

TWENTY-FIVE

⁓

By the time he walked to the center of the lobby, Jameson Frame felt as if the walls, the patrons and their clothing, even the light itself, had been drained of all color. He faced a small world in sepia, as if, in traveling in from the blustery outdoors, he had trekked through time as well.

He lurched to his right, toward the elevators. In passing through a group of rather agitated revelers, Frame saw a flash of leopard-print cloth too tight against pneumatic breasts and then, wretchedly discombobulated, collided with the hardened orbs. In reaching out to steady their possessor, he twisted himself downward to the floor, one leg intertwined against the other.

As he hit down with a quiet "Oofff," allowing the throb in his left leg to act as a springboard of sorts to get him to his knees, he saw, descending into the field of his vision, a hand with bright red nails, followed by a forearm that was braceleted from wrist to elbow.

He fluttered a hand in refusal, and turned to thank his Samaritan, only to hear, "Oh, Jameson, I thought that was you," followed by an achingly dramatic sigh.

The hand returned, insistent now, and hauled Frame up to his feet.

Righted, he said simply, "Vera."

And there she stood, eyes scanning as always, twin heat-seeking missiles.

"Jameson," she hissed, "you look terrible." And she seized him by the arm.

Saying farewell to the group of women that surrounded them, she steered Frame into the bar and seated him on a banquette that faced away from the door.

She signaled the waiter and mimed taking a swig and winked at him. Then she seated herself across from Frame, who looked at her with a single brow raised.

"That was just my Wiccan group. We meet every month for dinner and usually end up drinking here," she said, answering his unasked question. She tugged at a piece of her coarse hair that had unstuck itself from within the high-teased mass. She pushed the errant section back into place, pulled and removed invisible shafts of hair from between her teeth and scanned the room.

She flashed two jeweled fingers at the waiter and announced, "Two more," before he could lay his paper napkins on the table. And she took her black clutch from beneath one arm and laid it on the table.

"My God, let me look at you," she said in her husky voice and leaned forward to peer at him. She pressed his nose between her thumb and forefinger and turned his face into the dim overhead light.

"Well, the Masculane looks good, actually. You have that bumpy reaction, but that goes away. You don't need to worry about that. And the Botox . . . hmmmm. Frown, Jameson."

"I am," he said vaguely.

"Well, can't complain about that." She flicked at his chin, raising it.

"Lipo, too, huh?" she asked and he nodded against her hand.

"Are you in much pain?" she asked.

Frame nodded again.

"Where else?" she asked. "Lipo—where else?"

Frame pointed first to his stomach and then to either side of it. He moved his jacket aside so that she could see the spread of the red stain on his white shirt.

"Jeez, Jameson," she said. "Anything else?"

With a deliberate slowness that he thought perhaps he had learned from the boy who'd left him, he lifted his left foot to the edge of the bench upon which Vera sat, drew the fabric of his pants up over his ankle, up over his shin and finally, wincing at the pain of the slow-drawn lightweight wool, he unveiled his finished tattoo.

He studied it himself as Vera looked at it, and touched it with her cat's claw. He found himself rather admiring it, not having seen it before in its finished state. The simplicity of its message, the victorious V set in the perfectly rounded red circle, with the opening notes of Beethoven's Fifth, dot dot dot dash, interwoven. It was, to his eyes, a thing of simple, humble beauty.

But "that bastard," was all that he heard Vera say. "That fucking little cock-sucking bastard."

"He's gone now, you know," said Jameson Frame.

Vera looked up at him, while still spearing his V with a harpooned nail.

"Who?"

"That fucking little cock-sucking bastard," said Frame with a sad smile. "Gone."

"Well then good riddance, Jameson," said Vera as she grabbed the two shot glasses from the waiter before he had a chance to put them down in front of them.

"Two more," she told the waiter, before giving Frame a glass, clinking her own up against it and draining it in one quick gulp.

Frame studied her and then drank as well, draining his glass and gasping.

"Cuervo Gold," she said. "Drink some water."

He sipped his water and sighed.

"Anything else?" Vera asked him, studying his face.

"Any more procedures?"

Frame unbuttoned the top two buttons of his shirt and leaned forward, showing the wormy white flesh of his freshly shaved chest.

"Oh, for Christ's sake!" she said laughing and flicked her hand about inside his shirt, feeling the rough trail of razor burn and stubble left behind by the youth's unskilled manner. "You old fool!"

Frame found that word "old" sharp to his ears.

"When was the last time you slept?" she asked him. Considering, he shrugged slightly and looked at her with blank, heavy eyes.

She rummaged through her clutch.

"Well, here," she said, giving him a small bottle. "Take one, just one, mind you, at bedtime and I promise you, you will sleep. All you need's a good night's sleep, Jameson. And then you need to have a good talk with yourself. Think about what you're doing. You look like shit, Jameson. And you're much too old to be acting like this, running through the lobby like a mad man."

The drinks arrived. This time Vera pushed herself back from the table and allowed the waiter access. Then she said, "Please put the tab on the gentleman's room," and Frame fished in his pockets until he found his keycard, which he gave to the waiter.

The two clicked glasses again and drank. They drained their glasses in unison and set them hard on the table in perfect unison.

"Jameson," she said seriously, eyes suddenly dark, "maybe it's time you thought about going home. After all, the weather here is changing."

She reassured his hand with her own quick pat pat pat.

And she laughed then with the cackle of an old witch.

The waiter brought Frame back his keycard and his receipt and thanked them.

And they arose, and she pulled his face suddenly to hers and kissed him hard, pressing her bright red lips against his left cheek with an audible smack.

"Remember, Jameson, youth has only youth to offer," she said, as she flipped her platinum hair up over her head, patting it with a free hand.

"Need help getting up to your room?" she asked.

He shook his head "no" and she brought her fingers to her lips and gathered together a kiss and tossed it carelessly his way. And she turned then, and, smoothing the fabric of her very tight dress, walked off toward the canals.

Although Frame had found that he had welcomed Vera's company this evening, he could not bear the idea of her accompanying him to his room and, entering it, seeing the things that Chase had left behind. His old clothes shed, like a snake's skin, outgrown. His trash. His art, no doubt long since uploaded to his Internet site. His zip bag of drugs, which sat on the table by the bed. He wanted none of this seen, or, worse, reported back to Elsa.

Although the room had been cleaned during the day while they were gone, the wet mess of the bathroom, with mats and towels and clothing tossed about, marked a territory that was, in Frame's eyes, increasingly the boy's own.

Hearing a sound unlike the ocean's rhythmic roar, he went from the bathroom into the bedroom and saw that rains had begun. He opened the balcony door to the heavy Southern California rain. A heavy rain such as this, it seemed to Frame, only gave the massive ocean an opportunity to carve away at the tiny lip of the shore that, unnerved and exhausted, might fall away at last into the sea, dragging them all, the musclemen, the bike riders, the kite flyers, the tourists with fanny packs, and the mystics drumming at their interdimensional doorway, into the gray, arctic darkness of its belly.

He left the balcony door open, choosing his enjoyment of the sound of the rain pounding, pointlessly so far, against the balcony wall, over the safe enclosure of the sealed room. Frame took off his clothes and hung them carefully and put on his best pajamas.

He went back into the bathroom and straightened it, folding and hanging towels and wringing out mats. He went to the sink and, avoiding the sight of his own face, scrubbed his teeth and gently washed his face.

Leaving the light on over the sink, he left the room, pulling the door ajar to illuminate his bedroom.

He went into the living room and sat in front of his computer, turning it on. As the light on the screen grew, he switched it off again, suddenly feeling the weight of the drink, the exhaustion, and his terrible grief pressing down on his eyelids. He would, he thought, allow the waters of Venice this night to speak for themselves.

Back in the bedroom, he gathered up once more Chase's old clothes, the torn and stained things that he had worn when first they met. He folded them, neatly, almost gently, and placed them inside the top right drawer of the lovely mid-century bureau on the wall opposite the bed, happy to know that they were where they were and where they'd stay.

And he went back to the closet to retrieve from his suit pocket the pills that Vera had given him. Remembering her instruction to take only one, he swallowed two, laughing, and sat on the bed. He looked at the face of his exquisite watch, saw the passing of one day into the next, and then unbuckled the watch and set it on the table next to him. He then lay down, covering himself with the hotel's luxurious sheet, and closed his eyes, waiting for the pills to wash away the youth's face from where it had stained itself upon the inside of Frame's closed eyelids.

As he lay there, he felt the interaction of the drink and drugs, the ebb and flow of his myriad pains and listened to the roiling of his own troubled thoughts. With the passing of each moment, his presence of mind yielded a bit more to mere presence, until, at last, withstanding even the rustling of the curtains against the wind and rain sweeping in through the opened door, Jameson Frame fell into a deep sandpaper sleep.

TWENTY-SIX

⁂

Hours later, he came into a speckled form of consciousness, one in which, through the prisms of his eyes, shards of reality danced in front of him: Vera in a low-cut, much too small leopard-skin dress, Elsa loosing her scarf into the wind, and the boy, the youth, the one with the sumptuous skin sliding loosely, oh, too loosely over his own, as he washed him and stared into his hooded, night-colored eyes.

He felt a tug, a wrench, and felt himself cocooned, grasped very tightly, as if fitted to a straight jacket. And Frame awoke, in a room filled with a dismal green light, the sky the wind the rain still beating hard against the glass.

He moved to stretch and again felt the pull and realized in a moment of such pure horror that his immediate reaction was to laugh that, in the night, the flow from the adits, the punch holes in his skin, had allowed the bloody discharge to sink into the fine cotton of his pajamas and bind them, seal them against his skin, so that their removal was quite impossible.

He pulled at his pajama shirt as forcefully as he might, feeling an immediate deep agony, and let go, lying back, winded.

He turned his head, his chest still heaving with pain and with the realization of his entrapment and stared into the putty-colored sky, a sunrise like a sunset, a day like a long, oncoming night.

He listened for the sounds that the wind might bring him, of drums and shouts from the muscle men down the beach, or surfers vying for the best waves, of tourists, lost, as tourists always seem to be. He heard nothing, save nature. The wind and the waves, both overstimulated, overreaching.

And he lay there on the bed, alone and afraid, trapped in his finest pajamas and wondered where the boy could be, in wind and rain or in another's bed.

He pictured him, as he had, he suddenly realized, pictured him throughout the night and his chemical sleep, slowly taking off the coat of his new suit and the shirt, then the belt and the shoes and the pants, laughing, saying, "Look, see, see what the old fool has bought me. Soon I shall have his watch!"

Panicked, he sat up, feeling first the rip at his sides and then the sudden onset of new oozing, and reached for his bed stand and found his exquisite watch. He held it a moment, and, placing it with its face against the center of his forehead, he laid back down and fell again to sleep.

Awakening again to the same dead light, Frame hobbled into the bathroom, constricted in his movements by the glue of his own discharges and the pains that shivered up and down his limbs and all but incapacitated his breathing. He thought again of dinner and goodbye and shat and spat and got into the shower fully clothed and ran the water hot against his upturned head and let it run down his body, stinging, drenching and, ultimately, allowing him, with slow agony, to remove his pajama shirt and to step out of the bottoms that nearly had glued themselves to Frame's stubbly stomach.

With a deep sigh, he set the showerhead to a slow soft warm spray and inhaled the steam rising from the walls and floor. He kicked aside his wet pajamas and leaned against the tile, relaxing.

He ran the goat soap over the whole of his flanks, searching with his fingers to understand the worst of it. After feeling dozens of pinpricks of pain, he looked down to see the pinpricks of the adits, places where his skin had been hole-punched away, angry now, lit from within. Flipping slowly to turn his back to the spray, he rested his forehead against the cool tile, brought his bent arms up to help with support and rested there, gasping like an entrapped animal. He felt his heart pounding with odd irregularity in his chest and felt pain course down his arm, up into his jaw.

Before finishing, before turning off the water and stepping out into the relative chill of the room, he turned each wound in turn to the spray, taking the handheld wand and holding it against each field of pinpricks, with the hope of washing away, once and for all, the discharged mixture of blood and glue. He paid attention to his *Victory* tattoo, around which a mushroom head of a protrusion had formed.

Getting out of the shower, he happily grasped his thick, soft robe and allowed it to envelop him, before realizing the stains and stickiness that would result. But that likely had already begun. He tied the thing around him and wandered into the bedroom, where the damp of the storm filled the air. All around the huge window was a blanket of steam formed where the heat of the room met the open balcony door. The resultant fogged glass reminded Frame of the holidays at home, of the times in the cabin when the light of a single candle placed on the small drop leaf table by the window cut a circle of light into the icy window pane with similar results. And picturing his cabin in the woods now as a wonderful thing, a haven of warmth, of feasts, of all the ambered pleasantries of life, he reached quite quickly for his calfskin bag, placing it on the bed and feeling the rip in his side as he hoisted it down.

Jameson Frame sat on his California King, too sedated still to fill the suitcase, too weary even to close the balcony door, and felt, for a very long moment, an intense sense of self-pity. He leaned forward, his toes meshing with the deep pile of the carpet, his hands clasped each to the other, folded in his lap, his now taut chin dripping discharge on the collar of his fine white robe.

He fell asleep that way, his head nodding in deference to the evaporating anesthesia of the dilute lidocaine, and, in that shadow state, experienced a moment of bliss in which he, floating, walked weightlessly, soundlessly, and looked, when he faced himself in a mirror big enough to show the whole of him, nude, naked and unblemished, to be a figure of pure light. He felt in that moment the return to him of all the humors that had been drained away, with the discharge perhaps.

And within the shadow state, the figure of light whose facial features were diffused by the glow itself, laughed long and loud, showing teeth of pure white light in the reflective glass.

This time, when Frame awoke, he felt refreshed. He stood, found his legs steadier, and walked to the door to close it. But, instead, he walked out onto the balcony, feeling the air filled with sea spray and rain mixed, salt and fresh. He sat again as he had since the first day, on the little café chair behind the café table on his little balcony, and looked out to sea.

This day, no sun lit the sky.

The Pacific, no mirror, was, instead, an inscrutable thing, presence more than substance. A thing that, were you to attempt to hold it in your hands, you would find it instead to be holding you, lifting you up high for a giddy moment before the swallowing you whole and the long long drifting within its cold green muck. It called to him, in its roaring way. Teased him. Called him coward. It begged for penetration.

He got up, walked in, closed the door. He pulled the collar of his robe high against him, feeling the slickness of the spray against his skin. Suddenly, he felt quite hungry.

Finding hearty clothes among the many pieces of expedition wear that Elsa bade him buy, he pulled on a pair of heavily constructed jeans and a cotton turtleneck, knowing that a shower might be required to remove these as well. He found and wore heavy boots, a baseball cap and his exquisite watch. Armed with these and with a light waterproof jacket that he had brought with him in his suitcase, he gathered his things and went out for a walk in the rain.

The why of it struck Frame hard. Why, in spite of the storm at sea that rained onto the shore, the whole of Venice Beach, the whole of the cluttered rubble of it was swept away on a rainy day. Every kiosk was shuttered. Every tourist bused to safety. Every homeless creature hidden away in some crevice, housed in some shelter, gone. All gone, only the beach remained, like a long gray tongue thrust from the maw of the Pacific.

He walked along, his clothing wilting around him, the issue of his bodily glue resolved by nature. He sought, in his perambulation, a lamp lit, a bit of neon, a party hat to be had, maybe a burrito of the sort that Chase surely would have known how to find. In the air, no smells of cooking registered, no charcoals lit. Only the downpour and, in it, the void of festivities ended that lay in wait of festivities yet to come. He heard no music in the air, no clackety clack of skateboards nor the warning voices oncoming. Only this, only void.

He walked along, finding Santa Monica in the distance by the vague outlines of its white high rises, bleak against the smudged sky. Walked and walked as only a fool would, chilled and wet and tired and hungry, with a thousand aches and a million-pound heartache deep deep in his chest.

He walked until he felt like the swimmer who has swum out too far, who lacks the strength to kick and stroke his way back to shallow waters. Like the swimmer out beyond the line of breakers, looking back to the place where his journey began, he was, by now, a tiny pinpoint on the horizon, something that anyone seeking him would likely overlook.

He trudged a bit, looking to see the graceful façade of the Hotel des Bains somewhere in front of him, directly in front of his eyes, but he could not. It was not to be seen. Marooned, he rested instead, found the point of exhaustion in which not even his driving pain could drive him further, and threw himself down on a concrete bench with a huff.

Thirsty, he threw back his head and let the rain wash in. Hungry, he dreamed somehow of a mild chicken tikka masala, hot lamb vindaloo, matar paneer, and daal, simple daal, and was content.

He shivered in the rain as he curled up on his bench, tenting his little waterproof jacket over his head to relieve himself from the steady *pom-pom* of the ongoing rain pelting his skull under the cotton cap. And, for a time, he relaxed in his knowledge of the storm.

Wind came then, and sand swirled up around him, gouging his nostrils, his dishwater eyes, making him gather himself up and start again for the Hotel des Bains, his arms outstretched in sudden blindness.

The wind wracked him, taught him how deeply his body could feel a chill. How lonely a thing suffering was.

When he, at last, came upon the Hotel des Bains, he almost missed it, so intent was he on reaching some vague point on the horizon. Had the doorman not seen him, had he not rushed to his post at the door, which he had abandoned on this traffic-free day, had he not flung the door open and shrieked, "Mr. Frame," as loudly as he could against the chafing wind, the man would have surely passed by.

And yet, he heard the call and tottered into the foyer of the Hotel des Bains and blessed it and the doorman as he passed through and returned again to his hotel suite.

There he found again, as he always did, that even a moment's absence apparently was sufficient for the miracle, and that all had once again been put right in the room. All that was foul was swept way, or gathered up and binned. Fresh sheets, fresh towels, fresh soap and shampoo all welcomed him, as did the minibar freshly stocked, newly equipped for pleasure.

More, he saw, on the hotel telephone located by his bedside, that a round red light was flashing.

He stood in dumb show, watching it flashing flashing flashing, knowing and yet not knowing the meaning of the thing. Hoping beyond hope that he was in fact correct. That the phone call had come as promised.

"Can you get your town car?" It was Chase's voice, recorded. "Get it, okay?" He sounded highly agitated. There was a great deal of noise in the background.

"Get the car to come and get you and bring you to this address," Chase said before listing the address far too quickly for Frame to understand. Chase then stopped and, shouting over the ambient noise, said the address again, very slowly. He sounded as if he were under water.

There was the sound of a crash. And the boy said, "Fuck!" and covered the phone with his hand, muffling what he said thereafter. "Come, Jimmy, hurry," he shouted into the phone again. "We're making Big Art here, Jimmy, and I need you." The boy cried, his voice high with excitement.

"Oh," he screamed as Frame was beginning to return the headpiece to its cradle, "don't forget my camera. And bring the laptop, okay?"

His hands shaking, Frame took out his wallet, fanned out the business cards and called to order his town car.

In a warm change of clothing, Jameson Frame sat in the back of the town car as Anthony drove through the puzzle of the slick dark streets of Hollywood. More than once, he had had to back up and out of a one-way street or from the end of a dead-end road, cursing under his breath in Spanish.

As they drove now, Frame sat forward leaning into the driver's compartment, as both listened carefully to the automated voice of the GPS. At last, they arrived at what looked like the headquarters of a particularly seedy video-production company, whose signage announced "Hollywood Hot House" in scattered, broken-bulbed letters.

Anthony, who had heretofore driven Frame from his boutique hotel to Beverly Hills or the Hollywood Hills and back again, looked over his shoulder at the older man, as if to ask him if he was sure of the address of his destination.

Not sure that he would find a phone inside from which he could call his driver, Frame said only, "Come back in one hour, unless I find a way to contact you first?" and heard himself pitch his words as a question.

Anthony nodded and moved to open Frame's door.

"No, don't," said Frame, putting his warm hand fondly on his driver's forearm. "Stay in the car. There's no need."

And Frame ran out into the continuing downpour, skip-stepped aside a deep lake of water caused by a clogged drain and ran under the small awning and tried the door.

It was locked.

He pounded on the door and listened for movement within. In a moment, a young man with the look of a stoned skater about him opened the door, looking down at Frame from vexed, red-slitted eyes.

"Chase called me," he said, lifting the computer and camera into the pig-eyed youth's view. Frame noticed the scabs and whiteheads in the young man's wispy beard as the boy stood considering, before opening the door wide for Frame's entrance.

Frame nodded at his driver, who slowly backed away, stirring the lake of filthy water as little as possible as he exited the parking lot.

And Frame followed the boy into the place, ignoring the immediate stink of it and refusing to give over to the youth either the computer or camera. "Take me to Chase" he said in a ringing bark that startled them both.

They walked through a small workspace that was crowded with desks and above those desks with posters, each featuring in one way or another an engorged penis and a face—male or female or both, according to taste—twisted in lustful delight at the thought of what was to come. Titles like "Hollywood Honeys" and "Bubble Butts" stood out in red and yellow at the bottom of the posters.

In the corner, a leak on the roof stained the ceiling inside and dripped down in staccato drips in a green plastic bucket. Frame saw the contrast of the bucket against the cheap red indoor/outdoor carpet that filled the place. He watched the jalousie windows turned tight against the wind and rain, and wondered in what place Anthony would hole up for the hour.

In a coffee shop perhaps, with bitter coffee and terrible pie, or perhaps just in the car itself, parked in a quiet place, with the engine running for radio and heat?

Frame followed the boy through a dark passage, which led into an old studio in which lights clamped to the ceiling shown down on a platform in the center of the space. All around, Frame could make out faces in the darkness, and movement of cameramen as they recorded the action.

In the center of a pool of light, Chase lay back on a mound of pillows of every sort of color, his head thrown back, his legs outstretched and spread wide in front of him, cascading down the pile.

Between his legs bent a figure that Frame came to recognize as Kiki. Moving as close as he could without stepping into the light, Frame saw that Kiki, in elaborate eye makeup, jungle red lips and a chopped, spiked blonde Dynel wig on his head, had Chase's erect member thrusting into his mouth.

The noise of the entry interrupted Chase's trance and the irritated youth looked hard into the darkness around him.

The pig-eyed boy pushed Frame hard in front of him, bringing his face into the pool of light.

"Jimmy!" the youth said, pulling away from Kiki and climbing down off the platform.

Frame gave the computer and camera to the nude boy, who in turn gave it over to the pig-eyed boy, who took them and walked off into the dark edges of the room.

"It's time, Jimmy. We're making Big Art.

"I've been thinking about this a long time now, Jimmy," Chase said, excited, the heat of his nude form reviving the older man.

"Look, I've been like ultraprofessional since I met you. I've been working hard on my site to get my Chasers all excited about the new content so that I could find a way to monetize it all.

"And then I thought of it, Jimmy, the way I could do both, the way I could share myself with them all and the way they would all want to pay to see it. I mean, Jimmy, what's the one thing that the Chasers all want to do—suck me off, right? And so far I never did anything but wave my dick in their faces to keep them happy.

"So then it occurs to me to start thinking about the way that art is different from porn, the way you can be highly erotic but not porny, you know? And I thought that if I let some poor loser like Kiki suck my dick and recorded it, that would pretty much cross the line into porn. And no matter who sucked it, a guy or a girl, it would label me for that kind of sex and I would lose the other Chasers, which would be bad, in terms of money and art. So I thought about it and I just asked myself what Andy Warhol would do with the sucking part and the idea came to let them all suck me off, one at a time. Girls and guys and trannies, everybody. Come one, come all. And I put the word out on my site that I was making Big Art and they showed up and we've been recording ever since. As long as my dick holds out for the cum shot.

"Picture the video, Jimmy, all the cross cuts of their faces, the way that they first take me in their mouths, the looks on their faces, the way they suck, and the way that makes me feel. That's the important thing, I get that. One camera stays on my face the whole time, to give some reaction shots to cut to.

"Four cameras, Jimmy. *Four!* The whole thing's recorded. It's like the ultimate worship video, Jimmy. I'm like some Greek god up there, with the Chasers coming to worship. And I'm like some sacrifice as well, laid out before them to accept whatever they want to do. They can bite me if they want or refuse if they don't want to suck. But nobody refuses, Jimmy, when it's offered to them right there in all those bright lights with all those hungry mouths standing by. Everyone wants to taste me, Jimmy."

Frame began to take off his coat, his hat. He leaned against the platform as he listened to the boy's plan.

"This is the Big Art, Jimmy. This is where we take our time and show it all, show all the ways people react to getting what they want, all close-ups of desire played out on the screen. And it lets me be the one who gives them what they desire most and they, in turn, show me again and again how much they all desire me. All fade, cut, cut, cut, and slow dissolve."

He held an imaginary camera in front of him, running it up Frame's body to his face.

"This is where it all gets real, Jimmy."

"So, what? You want me to watch?" asked Frame. "Or do you want me to run the fifth camera for you, write dialogue, what?"

The youth, somewhat taken aback, turned his twilight eyes to Frame.

He brought his lips close to Frame's ear. The older man felt warm breath against his skin.

"Don't you get it, Jimmy? I want you to be in it."

It seemed for a moment as if every function in Frame's body—respiration, heartbeat, vision, hearing—all came to a standstill. As if, like sexual climax, the boy's words referenced a "little death."

"You can't possibly believe"—Frame began, before losing the power to speak to his choked tongue.

"Jimmy," said the boy, moving his face in front of Frame's. "Jimmy, nobody's ever wanted me more than you." And he stepped closer, allowing the older man to feel the hardness of the erection that lay between them.

"Take it," said the boy. And Frame did so, took hold of the boy's member.

"Hold it," said Chase, kissing the back of Frame's neck. "Squeeze it," he said, biting down on the flesh.

"Suck it, Jimmy. I need it, man. No matter who is watching."

Their faces close, they breathed the warmth of each other's exhalation. The boy ran his open lips and tongue along the man's mouth, face and neck.

"Suck me, Jimmy," Chase begged, his voice cracking with lust. "Make me come."

And the boy took the man out to the platform, where a hidden switch suddenly brought an amber hue to the lights. The youth turned his naked ass to the man as he clambered to the top of the cushions. The man responded by going to the bottom of the bed, putting one knee up and hoisting himself forward and up.

"Go," was all that Chase said, before seating himself on the cushions above and nodding to Frame to climb up to his outspread legs.

The sound of someone, Bobo perhaps, slapping out some systolic rhythm on his bongo drums somewhere in the back, in the dark that prowled the corners of the room, where the skater boys were and the girls with Kohl eyes, and the older men and women, some whose faces, what snatches Frame saw of them, wore masks of lonely need, others whose eyes burned with lust.

He was shoved toward the boy, who was himself writhing upon his padded throne, an old hospital bed stripped of its sides, bedizened with a crazy quilt of hand-tinted rags, batiks, spangles and garlands gathered from attics and holidays past. Holiday lights were strung about, lit, twinkling, insinuating the nighttime sky. Under the quilt of many colors were mounds of pillows, raising up the youth's body, making for him a nest of clouds, so that the cameras shooting him from below would point upward, from sole to balls to armpit to brow, in recording him. So that he and he alone was presented as the oblation, with all others as supplicants, as devourers, sucking, quite literally sucking the life out of him.

Frame found his face nearly pressed into the mound of fur that covered the youth's groin, found himself welcomed within striking distance of his tumescent cock, his pendulous balls. Found his air of hesitation still fully intact. The wall of *nonononononononononono* foremost on his mind, and yet . . . And yet he sensed the yearning delicious sense of *yyyesssss*, reminding him that, just this once, just this one time in the whole timeline of his stifled life, he need only, to be utterly and hopelessly happy, to let go. Need literally to only nod his head, mouth open.

And he did. Like leaping whole into the vast puzzle of the ocean, he submerged his face into the boy, first resting and breathing him in, and then writhing along as the body beneath him moved his torso, his crotch, his legs in a slow undulation. He then kissed him softly, later sloppily and insistently and then by placing his mouth on the tip of his prick and kissed it and drank it in and then drank deeper, sucking it whole.

The sense of the forbidden surged in him, and a surprising sense of communion as well. He looked up at Chase's face, at his thundercloud eyes, and discovered nothing within them, but took what was given, took that which he had wanted, took it and took it and took it and was satisfied.

His hands sculpted his lust. He held Chase hard, first against the pubic bone and then, thumbs plowing the rings of muscles in the abdominal wall, upward, driving to the navel, reaching for the waist. Then he drew his hands down, clawing the boy's skin, hearing his gasp, feeling him quiver as he drew his hands down to the inside of the boy's thighs. Here his face met his hands, and, as his fingers pressed the darkness behind the balls, his teeth scraped the soft inside of the thigh, gently at first and then with sharp vigor. And Chase cried out, having lost all sounds save the gutterals.

He held the youth's balls, cradling them with his hand, brought his face to them, kissed them, licked, swallowed them, first the one and then the other.

He fell upon the youth's erect dick again and sucked it deeply enough that he began to feel a sense of gagging begin to build in the back of his throat. In response, he took it deeper, letting desire overwhelm the choking.

Jameson Frame felt whole, felt full, felt completed in that moment. And something more, he felt, far from the weak-kneed, yielding, debased, aged fool that he feared he would be, he felt powerful, controlling, not controlled. Chase writhed under his every touch, turned and was led like a brood horse with the simple touch of the reins. Time and again he felt the boy harden within him, responding to his insistent rhythm. And time and time again, he slowed or lightened his touch, pushing back the youth's release and listening to his pelting moans.

In these moments, he noticed the increased attention of the cameramen running the four cameras, as they drew in close for the money shot. He noticed again how they slunk back, disappointed, as he refused to give the boy his exit.

Frame raised himself up at once to plunge his face into Chase's stomach, and licked his navel. He slowly moved his face downward again, feeling the slickness of his own spit, down the boy's treasure trail and again through his bush, feeling the engorged cock slap against him again and again.

He played with the tip of the cock, purpled with desire, felt the sponge of it go hard as steel, droplets of thick, clear fluid forming at the lip.

And he lay below it finally, feeling the full heat of the thing resting against his face, thinking again *yyessss*, the final yes.

And he took it and strangled it in his mouth.

Chase stammered, "I'm gonna come. Jimmy, I'm gonna come," and he tried to pull his cock away, to show the fountain that was building inside him to all the four cameras.

The boy's toes curled, his body bucked, and Frame dove deeper, wanted more and, when the moment came, swallowed hard before pulling back and letting the cameras find the trail of pearlescent white discharge that he spit out on Chase's chest, all to the sounds of the boy's gagging moans as he clutched at the fabric all around him.

Slowly, Frame pulled back, lifted up and kneeled there, wiping the rest away from his mouth with the back of his hand. As he pulled back slowly, Chase, just as slowly, extended his arm out to the older man.

Were there tears in the young man's eyes, in his bewildered eyes? There were, of course, in the older man's.

Ignoring the stain in the front of his own pants from where he himself had come during his long, long exploration of the young man's dick, Frame arose then, sobbing from joy, relief, anger, experience, and sorrow. Sobbing from the loss of all that he had lost and walked into the darkness as the drummer who was perhaps Bobo let the rhythm that he beat on the drums fade into a few last erratic taps on the drums' skin.

The cameramen set down their cameras and the artists who lurked outside the shot, waiting their turns or already regretting them, began to mill about as well. The buzzing of whispers grew as the smell of fresh sex grew more diffuse.

His coat back on, Jameson Frame, his hand up to the top of the closed collar, pulling it even tighter to his throat, waited for his town car. Waiting, he was left alone. No one approached, not Chase or his Chasers. Instead, he waited to see the familiar headlights, whose flash from high to low to high again would signify his return to the Hotel des Bains.

When the car arrived, Frame hurried out and seeing the rain unabated, climbed into the back of the town car, and allowed his head to loll against its rest. And the two were silent, both of them, sensing somehow the inadequacy of words.

TWENTY-SEVEN

⟨≈⟩

By midnight, the storm had gathered into an entity. It called to him from beyond the glass wall. It invited him to come and dance.

Jameson Frame sat on his California King, his hand on the handle of his calfskin bag. He sat, imperious, puffing a reefer. What was left in the room from the boy's zip lock was scattered across the top of the bed.

His clothing stuck to his skin once more. His *Victory* leg leaked pus on the carpet. The nodes by his eyes whirled agony directly into his mind, whorled his vision into sparks of light in kaleidescoped primary colors in a world otherwise comprised of bickering shadows. He kept the lights off now, for the sake of his eyes, and for the avoidance of reflection. On entering his suite, he had covered all mirrors with fluffy clean towels, as if he were sitting shiva. He took that part of his shirt that was stuck to his stubbly torso just over his pounding chest and tore at it, ripping it not only apart, but also away from his inflamed heart as well; he gasped from the pain, then laughed, the ritual now complete.

Where, he wondered, was his "meal of comfort," cooked by loved ones out of concern? There being none of those, he did not eat, but waited, as if expecting the Kaddish to be spoken for him. Given him in a dream. God, he knew, in the saying of it was many things: great, powerful, loving, wise—perhaps some, perhaps all. And more. But distant, most certainly that, and that goes without saying, without remembrance.

He knew that, emerging from the fog of the drug, there would be hunger, but he had learned all about hunger and where it got him.

The storm sang to him again, from the cracks around the balcony door where the wind slipped in, in a voice with too much vibrato. Sang to him a familiar song. From *The Magic Flute*, surely. Surely. He knew he recognized it. And he was sure that what he heard was his only love, the Queen of Night, flinging her *Der Hölle Rache kocht in meinem Herzen* out, tongue unrolling at him on the high note.

How apt, he thought, *how fitting*. "Hell's vengeance boils in my heart."

Shall I dine then on my own boiled organs? He giggled at the prospect.

Feeling some new wetness on his face, he wondered about the presence of some new discharge, but, pondering the nature of things, settled instead on the possibility of tears.

A few minutes later, he asked himself how much lidocaine would likely be enough? He had, however, no answer to give himself, and so he lit the butt of his joint from where it had given off its last spark, somehow smudging the edge of his comforter, burning through without igniting it, and took another puff.

His feet were gone now, quite gone. Misplaced. Frame was now working to account for his hands and mouth.

Another time, Frame attempted to remember just who it was, aside from himself, who carried the weight of the world on his shoulders. Hercules, he knew, did the trick for a moment only and yet called it one of his Great Labors. But whose job was it every day?

Atlas. The word spun round to him, a letter at a time, like the fruit in a slot-machine's screen. *A.T.L.A.S.*

And then he cried some more, making noises like a mistreated hound.

At some point in the night, he ordered a twenty-dollar hamburger from room service and found, to his rancorous dismay, that he had to order fries separately. He asked for it to be cooked medium, just barely pink, as he thought pink was all he could abide, and for cheese as well—cheddar he thought, but only if the cheddar they had was a good one. Nothing that had been presliced and packaged in plastic. Assured that it was only the best from the kitchen of the Hotel des Bains, he ordered it with everything and asked for a hot-fudge sundae to boot, with a pot of coffee on the side.

He had decided to watch the storm all the way to the end.

Waiting for his food, he happened upon the idea of dragging his beloved little café table from the balcony into the suite and placing it right in front of the glass wall, giving himself a front-row seat. He flung open the door, which smashed in against the wall, marring it with the doorknob and sounding like a gunshot round. He ran onto the balcony, and, instantly soaked, got his little café chair and pulled it in. The table proved harder, the round top a little wider than the door.

Using all his remaining strength, he lifted the table, unsure in that moment whether to drag it in, angling it to clear the doorway, or simply throw it off the balcony and be done with it.

He pulled it inside, his chest heaving. Bent over the top of the table, he considered simply dropping himself there, to be found by the food-service waiter. Instead, powered by the idea of such a wretched exit, he pushed himself up off the top of the table, standing, and, quite without thinking, ran onto the nearly empty balcony, overturned the one remaining chair and rested his right foot on it, crying:

Blow, winds, and crack your cheeks! Rage! Blow!
You cataracts and hurricanoes, spout
Till you have drench'd our steeples, drown'd the cocks!

(He stopped, gasping a bit for air, and listening for a knock at the door, laughing at the use of that word, "cocks," before continuing at full voice, aimed out at the ocean and sky)

You sulphurous and thought-executing fires,
Vaunt-couriers to oak-cleaving thunderbolts,
Singe my white head! And thou, all-shaking thunder,
Strike flat the thick rotundity o' the world!

Quieted by exhaustion and by the choice of being Lear in the storm or the comforting fool, he hurried back into the room, slamming the door with trembling arms.

Only then was he aware of the knocking at the door in the outer room.

"Just a moment," he called, his voice sounding unnaturally high.

He hurried about, finding his soft white robe, which had been hung again for him on the back of the bathroom door and turning on a single light in the sitting room as he passed by. He opened the door, bowing slightly to the young waiter and asking him to put his tray on the desk in the front room. He stood blocking the man's view into the bedroom as he waited and then signed the chit, giving the man a king's ransom of a tip.

"Thanks for all your many kindnesses," he said to the young man as he closed the door in his face.

And he ate. He ate with his full desire for survival. He bit into the burger on its artisanal bun and found it good and bloody and nearly cold, but he ate. Without catsup, because he could not wait to open the little bottle. He did pour the whole packet of the yellow mustard onto his plate and drag his burger in it before each bite.

He ate the fries, not one by one, but in bunches, punching them into his mouth, his throat attempting to swallow them before his teeth could chew them. He dragged them, too, in the mustard, until it was gone.

He loved the flavors as they coated his throat, filled his stomach, the grease, the salt. When all else was gone, he dragged the lettuce, bit by bit, through the blood on the plate and ate, until all was gone.

But then there was the coffee, hot, strong, bitter. And the sundae.

Remembering this, he took them into the bedroom and set them upon the café table and uprighted the chair. He poured a cup of coffee with the same ennui of the most polished waiter and sat, stirring sugar into his cup and lifting the ice cream in its dish up to his lips and drinking down the melted part.

He moaned aloud when he tasted the first spoonful of ice cream and fudge. He stared out into the vast endlessness of the endless night and swallowed the rich combination of the contents with joy. It quivered his thighs, the cold, the hot, the sweet and sticky. And he kissed the cold glass bowl. When empty, he licked the bowl, sticking his tongue down and around for the chocolate. And he placed it quite daintily on the top of the table.

Only the coffee left, he sipped at it, hoping that it might, in some way, restore him to the man he once was. He thought of the coffee at his cabin, of Grace setting it before him at his own dining room table, some book or other propped up against the sugar bowl. How he barely glanced at her or it, but fixed it by rote, sugar, milk, not cream, and sipped at it restoratively.

He drank it all, his being turning to acid as he did.

Clutching at his gut, he thought of Dorothy Parker in a rush:

What fresh hell is this?

He laughed again, giving his mind free rein to roam about. *Think about everything but what there is to think about,* he instructed himself.

He wondered aloud for a moment where the table and chair might have come from and then fretted over whether or not he would sleep after drinking so much coffee.

And he went over to the bedside table and dug at it with his hands until he found the little bottle of pills that Vera had given him.

He took two, swallowing with a dry throat and choking as they stuck. And he went into the bathroom, stuck his head under the faucet and drank, swallowing them down. Tired, he sat on the toilet, his arm up on the tank, his legs crossed in front of him, his big toe bobbing, still clutching Vera's bottle in his hand.

In the passage of time, while he was still sitting on the toilet, the burning in Frame's stomach turned to churning, then deep nausea. He felt the sick rising in the back of his throat and was glad of his throne as he knelt before it and vomited once, twice. He raised his head back from the second attack, a slim thread of mucous hanging from his mouth. And he gagged again on the rising bile rushing upward, pouring outward from him, some into the toilet and some onto the bathroom's elegant tile floor.

He did not look away, but looked into the mess, as if attempting to glean meaning in entrails. What he saw, or thought he saw was blood. Not a great deal, but enough to dye some of the rest a raspberry red.

When he saw that some had landed on his robe and clothes, he staggered to the shower and turned the dial, allowing the water to spray in scalding intensity. And he threw himself in, soaking the clothes, the robe, his skin, his hair, feeling the burn against his burning skin. He heard his own breathing, rapid, shallow, almost a rattle and calmed himself with calming words:

Blessed are the poor in spirit, for theirs is the kingdom of heaven.
Blessed are those who mourn, for they will be comforted.
Blessed are the meek, for they will inherit the earth.

He walked out of the shower and picked up Vera's bottle from where he had laid it on the toilet tank.

He walked over to the sink, lifted the bottle to his lips and upturned it, ready to swallow all. He found only a single pill. He brought his disappointed face down to the faucet once more and swallowed it down.

As an afterthought, he smeared toothpaste on the side of his index finger and ran it again and again across his filthy teeth, minting the bile on his tongue. He rubbed his whole mouth quickly and then swished water through it and spit it out. He wiped his chin on the towel over the mirror and staggered out of the bathroom, his evening toilet routine complete.

Exhausted, he walked slowly into the bedroom and made his way slowly to the California King and, dropping himself on it with the last of his conscious strength, he wrapped his nude body within the soft top sheet, *thinking let this be my shroud*, not caring whether he glued himself to the thing or not.

And that was his last conscious thought.

He saw only one thing more, in the dead of night, when the storm produced a bolt of lightning so bright that it lit the world. And Jameson Frame woke from his wooden slumber to see the apocalypse. With burning eyes, he witnessed the majesty of God for the briefest of moments and heard the voices of angels roaring after, as the tablets were rent. And the lambs and goats were separate.

And he fell asleep once more, not sure of what had happened.

TWENTY-EIGHT

⁓

Jameson Frame awoke illuminated, the room filled with color and light. He looked at his hands rising out of his shroud, the blood and bones playing beneath the skin with the radiation all around. Never had a morning been so bright and never had Frame felt so enlightened.

One more fragment of verse unearthed itself in his mind, the find of an ancient era, a lonely one that featured stormy storms and foolish stupid, smelly seamen:

> *The Mariner, whose eye is bright,*
> *Whose beard with age is hoar,*
> *Is gone; and now the Wedding-Guest*
> *Turned from the bridegroom's door.*
>
> *He went like one that hath been stunned,*
> *And is of sense forlorn:*
> *A sadder and a wiser man*
> *He rose the morrow morn.*

Frame banished Coleridge, in a flash, falling back on his *On Scrimshaw and Others* for succor. Never had such a morning such an Easter cheer. As he had, in fact, himself risen, *risen* on that *morrow morn*, a sadder and wiser man.

He tugged at his sheet and, to his great and simple delight, found that it fell away with a little snap, that his discharges were, perhaps, discharged, the diluted toxins had perhaps at last flushed away.

He went into the bathroom to relieve himself and smelled the cadaverous mess before he saw it. Ashamed, he wanted to throw the sheet over it, but, instead, went to his wallet and, emptying it of every bill, placed that and a note written on the back of a hotel envelope saying "Sorry" on the top of the lid.

He went from the loo to stand by the glass wall of the room, to look on his day. Never before had he seen such a sumptuous sky, or so he felt. Clear azure, pure blue, majestic in his view. The ocean beneath had been tamed by the sky. After days of rising up, of turbulent roiling, of threatening, it laid there, placid. Pacific. Calm. Waiting for the full swing of the sun to enlighten it, to send from it searchlights into the sky.

He wondered in that moment what Kyle and the Ghoul would make of them, this sea and this sky, when they looked out, arrested by the beauty of their jetliner view, standing with Kyle in panties and the Ghoul hooded like a wizened monk on the redwood deck of their cantilevered retreat in the bird streets.

He wondered also what tickling sounds were being issued from Elsa's throat when she awoke that morning. What peculiarly foreign joys entered her head with the sight of the butterfly bushes luring so very many bees.

He pictured Vera in a negligee then, gauzy and short, with feathered mules and her hair clipped up, but falling in a veil of soft, loose curls, all around the huge black-framed sunglasses that she wore while sipping a Bloody Mary, hot with Tabasco.

And he asked with all his heart, picturing a lantern-shaped jaw with a black gauzy beard, what philosophy possessed the youth who in turn still possessed his heart and he heard him speak, disembodied, in his squeaky voice,

"I think you've got to fuck hard and make a lot of noise doing it."

And he didn't know, hearing this, if he had supplied these words and put them in Chase's mouth, or had actually heard him say it.

So his love, he feared, began receding into memory. The thought of it brought hot tears to his eyes. And the thought of it relieved him, as he ran his hands over the safe, dead hide of his calfskin bag.

He realized that, even given the opulent brightness of the day, the hour must be early, as the sun, raining down on him from over his hotel's shoulder, had yet to clear downtown Los Angeles.

And he looked at the exquisite watch that, in spite of it all, was still clipped hard to his wrist, and he saw, to his deep delight, that the day had just begun. And, if he hurried, before it ended, he could be at home.

The day was one for daffodils, he considered, and then thought that all poets had their daffodils, Eliot again, in *Intimations,* where he gave an unhappy skull specified flower bulbs instead of eyes. Or Wordsworth, better still, who danced with them, who saw them with such joy that, when they were gone from him, the joy of remembering was joy enough. And Jameson Frame hoped that, *when oft and on his couch I lie / in vacant or in pensive mood*, for him as well the joy of remembrance of joy would be joy enough.

Surely. Surely.

He would find a way that very day to test the theory, to gather in his hands bunches of the butter-yellow flowers.

And yet there was something of a chill in the plumbing of his heart when he realized it.

The distance in miles.

The distance in time.

The boy one day soon coming to his hotel room, calling Jimmy Jimmy and knocking expectantly, butterflies jumping in his greedy heart, and finding the old man was gone. Retreated to an unreachable Olympus, his body mending by the taste of malt, the scent of leather and touch of old wood.

He went then, and took the towel down from his bedroom mirror and studied himself again as he stood naked before it.

What he saw there, the devil that overtook his renewed sense of calm, was the sight of himself as an oversized doll. The image of him as molded by Mattel.

He saw the whole of it then, the wardrobe, the artifice as all of a piece, complete with suite to store him in.

No line, no mar, only things smooth and supple. Unnatural.

Immediately he packed his calfskin suitcase with only the things that had come west with him. He dressed himself in a simple pair of khakis and a white cotton shirt and slipped his feet in his old slip-ons. The rest he hung meticulously in the closet positioning all by color, the new shoes left on the top shelf, all in a row. Except for the things, the boy's things, rags really. Those he left neatly folded in the darkness of the drawer. And he called down to the desk to ask them to send a bellboy right up to get his bag for him.

In the time remaining, he put the table and chair back on the little balcony and saw to it that each was placed just so. And then he closed that door behind him tight.

He stood once more for one last time in front of the glass wall, looking out to sea. To where the tendrils of light were just now touching, resulting in a fog of light arising from the foam. He heard it roaring in his heart and felt the need one last time to walk the sand.

He left the door ajar, with the suitcase holding it open, and, passing the bellboy in the hall, asked him to take it down and store it behind the front desk.

Downstairs, at the desk, in a hurry, he asked for help securing his town car for the trip to the airport and arranged for a ticket on the first plane home that had a first-class seat available. And thanking all, and gesturing by turning his pockets inside out that all ready cash was gone, he hurried out the front of the Hotel des Bains, saw the boardwalk in the last moments before it awakened, coming out of hiding from the storm, and, having no impediments, walked briskly across to the beach.

The marvel of it, pure white, scoured clean, each needle, bag and bottle dragged into the great wet abyss beyond. The immaculate scent of clean ocean air. He leaned down and touched the beach, patted it, a living thing, and felt a feeling of lightheadedness as he raised his head. The sea before him seemed a sun of sorts itself now as the day grew upon it.

Jameson Frame was dazzled, bewildered, aghast. He raised a bended arm in front of his eyes, guarding himself. He moved a few paces down toward the sea.

He stood in the place of the sukkah and felt its tug, felt the tug in his heart, the opening of wounds. The unraveling of what had been knit up tight. The yearning, the magnificent, voluptuous yearning.

He felt pain again, worse than the pain he'd felt all these days. Felt pain as if the word *pain* were a new word, with a new weight and tang. Felt his legs as hollow things, splintering, his strong arms a wispy memory. He toppled in the sand, a heavy useless mass.

And he knew that, in his wanderlust, he had grown an indigenous heart.

His last wish was to see, just once more, that pair of eyes that held twilight at the height of day.

His body, a great rag doll dropped carelessly in the sand, was found sometime after, when the world came out to play.

Later, in seeking the cause of death, they noticed his heart was quite empty, bloodless, as if drained by a million cuts.

Perhaps the notice in the papers, "Sudden Loss of a Man of Letters," or the entire hour of television time, with the roundtable show dedicated to remembrance of his life and work, as an actress of some note with black-rimmed glasses perched on the end of her nose reading from *On Scrimshaw and Others*, would have pleased him, even though Gore Vidal refused to take part.

Perhaps it was, as Elsa would insist, that he was pulled through layers of reality as he lay there on that beach, swallowed by some conniving universe.

Or, as Vera saw it, a waste, a terrible fucking waste.

Or perhaps it was as the youth saw it, one less Chaser in pursuit.

He hurried his *Big Art* up onto his Internet site and thought of the loss as merely the thing that happened next in the long chain of events that happened in his young life. He wished, though, that he'd asked for the exquisite gold watch that Jimmy had worn, as he knew that he surely would have gotten it as something to remember him by.

In his last moments, lying helpless in the cold wet deserted sand, his heart burning out inside him, Jameson Frame spoke his last to the sun, as it came up on him from over the hotel, as it blinded him, as everything around him fried white.

He died cursing, *fuck fuck fuck*ing the light, as he groped in vain for the sunglasses that he had abandoned up above in his suite in the Hotel des Bains, where the housemaid who had had to scrub up his sick helped herself to them after pocketing her tip and muttering *repugnante*, tucking them into the thick braided hair on top of her head, wanting nothing more herself than to walk out into the sun, and, pulling them down into place over her twilight blue eyes, enjoy the bohemian freedom of a sunny day on the boardwalk lining Venice Beach.